Bernardin de Saint Pierre

PAUL & VIRGINIE

Translated from the French

by

Raymond HEIN

EDITIONS DE L'OCEAN INDIEN

© RAYMOND HEIN (1976)

> *"Owing to the insertion of a sentence at the wrong place, in the Introduction to our first Edition, the translator has been made to say that M. Mahé de Labourdonnais was Governor of Isle de France when Bernardin de St. Pierre arrived in 1767."*
>
> *"In fact, M. de Labourdonnais had left 20 years sooner, and had died in France in 1753."*
>
> *"This sentence should have been inserted at the following page of the Introduction to that Edition, at line 26, indicating that M. de Labourdonnais, as stated by Bernardin de Saint Pierre, was the Governor in August 1744 when the Saint Géran was lost."*

Published by

**Editions de l'Océan Indien
Stanley, Rose-Hill, Mauritius.**

1st Reprint : **Henry & Co** (1981)
2nd Reprint : **Regent Press** (1985)
3rd Reprint : **Kin Keong Printing, Singapore** (1992)

THE AUTHOR

Raymond Hein needs little introduction. Besides being an eminent figure in the legal profession, a distinguished humanist moulded by Professor Bowra of Oxford University, he is well-known in literary circles and for more than half a century has played a very important role in our national life. His translation of *Paul et Virginie* is among the best English versions of the novel that has been published. In it, he succeeds not only in describing and depicting the original thoughts and ideas of the book but also in reflecting the originality of the text.

The first edition of the book, published in 1977, was a notable contribution to Mauritian literature in English, and has been so successful that this new edition has become necessary.

Another book by Raymond Hein, *Le Naufrage du St. Géran*, inspired by Bernardin de Saint Pierre's book, has been published in France. This work required a considerable amount of research on the part of Raymond Hein, as he was concerned to differentiate the reality of the shipwreck from the legend, an aim which he achieved with complete success. This book is the first ever published about the dramatic saga of the ship on which Virginie, the famous and touching heroine of Bernardin de Saint Pierre, is made to die.

Beneath the groves where on that fateful day
Virginie's youthful frame was laid to rest,
The lonesome traveller on his rambling quest
May pause a while leaving the noisy fray.

The old church stands where she was wont to pray
And birds live on that in her trees still nest;
Her memory of time has stood the test,
Haunting these woods where love once shed its ray.

But all is gloom — there dwells but sadness here,
And through the tropic nights one oft can hear
'mid crashing waves a vessel torn apart,

While roams a vision pale in maiden form
With eyes to heaven raised beyond the storm,
Her lover's image press'd against her heart.

                                                          RAYMOND HEIN

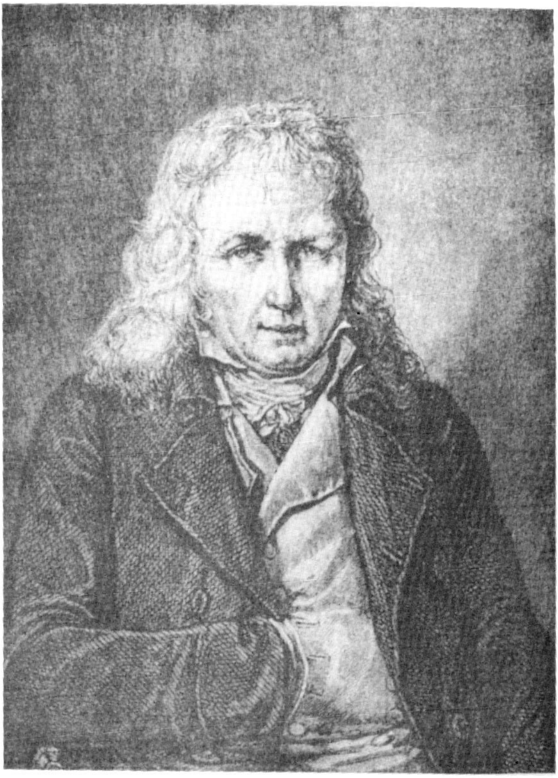

INTRODUCTION

Jacques Henri Bernardin de Saint-Pierre was born at Le Havre on the 19th of January 1737.

Inspired by the reading of Robinson Crusoe, he travelled to Martinique at the age of twelve, and returned, disappointed, to join a school run by Jesuit priests in Caen, and, later, a College in Rouen.

In 1760, as a military engineer, he took part in the Seven Years' War in Germany. The following year he was sent to Malta on a geographic mission. Between 1762 and 1766, he visited Holland, Russia, Poland, Austria.

It was in 1767 that, while on a mission to Madagascar, he came to the Isle de France, as Mauritius was then called.

Here, the author stayed for several years, collecting the material for this famous novel which he wrote after returning to France, and which was first published in 1788.

In 1793, he married Félicité Didot, daughter of his publisher, and, the following year, his daughter Virginie was born. A son, Paul, was born to them in 1798.

Félicité died in 1799, and, a year later, he married Désirée de Pelleporc, more than forty years his junior.

In spite of the wide difference in age, their marriage was an extremely happy one.

A follower of Napoléon Bonaparte, he was made a member of the Legion of Honour in 1806. He was elected to the French Academy, whose presidency he assumed in 1807. He died in Eragny on the 21st of January 1814.

A statue of Bernardin de Saint-Pierre by David d'Angers is to be seen at Le Havre and, another, representing him with Paul and Virginie, at the Jardin des Plantes in Paris. In Mauritius, a bronze group representing Paul carrying Virginie across the river, the work of the famous Mauritian sculptor Prosper d'Epinay, is to be found in the gardens of the Municipality of Curepipe. A marble replica of the same group belongs to the Municipality of Port Louis.

The theme of the pastoral romance was not pure invention on the part of the author. A vessel, the *Saint Géran*, in fact sank off the north east coast of the Isle de France, some distance from Ile d'Ambre, in the night of the 17th to the 18th of August 1744.

The Governor was then François Mahé de Labourdonnais, founder of the City of Port Louis, of whom Lord Macaulay speaks as " a man of eminent talents and virtues ".

The wreck of the vessel was discovered and identified some ten years ago, lying outside the coral reefs near what is known as 'la passe des Citronniers'. The *Saint. Géran* had left the port of Lorient on the 24th of

March under the command of Captain de la Mare or Delamarre, with 186 persons on board, including the crew.

She picked up another 30 on the way and some had died before she ran into the coral reefs off Isle d'Ambre where she sank early on the 18th of August. Most of the passengers went overboard in an attempt to swim to shore. Three girls, Miss Caillou, Miss Mallet, and Miss Neizein were among the passengers. One of the Officers, Mr. Longchamp de Montendre tried to persuade Miss Caillou to come with him. Whether she agreed or not is not known, but they both perished. A member of the crew, in vain tried to persuade Captain de la Mare to divest himself of his clothes without which, he explained, he stood a better chance of survival. The latter stubbornly objected that he could not decently reach the shore in the nude, and besides, that he had the custody of certain papers which he could not leave behind. He chose to try and escape on a raft; but was drowned. From this incident, testified to by the survivors, the author conceived the touching image of Virginie refusing to undress, even if her refusal was to cost her her life.

"This transformation", writes Anatole France, "is "typical of the genius of the author, whose imagin-"ation softens, embellishes and feminizes every "circumstance."

Acknowledged in France as a masterpiece from the time of its first publication, this novel soon won the admiration of readers all over Europe. New editions appeared, year after year, as well as translations in English, Italian, Spanish, Portuguese, Greek, Armenian, Hungarian, Dutch, Russian and other languages.

In Mauritius, the memory of Bernardin's pure heroine has been cherished and preserved over the ages by a modest monument in Pamplemousses Botanical Garden, across the road from the church where Madame de la Tour and Virginie attended mass on Sundays.

Whether this monument was erected to her memory — or whether it is only part of an altar built in honour of the pagan deity, Flora, by a French Governor of the Isle de France, as Pierre Benoit asserts,— Virginie, all Mauritians will agree, survives in these surroundings.

Of all that has been said or written in praise of Bernardin de Saint-Pierre's work, may we just reproduce this one extract from Patin's "Eloge de Bernardin de St. Pierre" ?

"Never yet, I dare affirm, have more charming "scenes of happiness and virtue been combined "in one single work with a truer description of humble "everyday life; it is the faithful rendering of this "simple and homely morality which causes the almost "ideal perfection of that evangelical moral to appear "to us so acceptable. It is the truth of its ethics, "which, to my mind, is the foremost merit of "Paul

"and Virginie" and the complete eulogy of this work
"is to be found in the naive words of the Governor,
"when under the spell of these happy families he
"exclaims : "All the furniture here is of wood, but
"the countenances are serene and the hearts of gold."

And, again, "What names could be more pleasing
"to us", Patin asks, "than those of Paul and
" Virginie ? "Are there any which call back to our
"hearts sweeter and more touching recollections ?
"Who does not recall the games and the affection
"of these amiable children ? Who does not remember
"with sorrow the story of their cruel separation and
"of their tragic end ?"

FOREWORD

I have formed ambitious designs in this small work. I have attempted to describe a land and a flora different from those of Europe. Our poets have long enough set their lovers on the banks of streams, in meadows and in the shade of beech trees. I wanted to set mine on the sea shore, at the foot of rocks in the shade of coconut, banana or lemon trees in blossom. The southern worlds only lack poets like Theocritus and Virgil to present us with pictures at least as interesting as those of our country. I am aware that travellers, men of taste, have given us enchanting descriptions of several of the South-sea isles; but the ways of their inhabitants and more especially those of the European settlers often spoil the scenery. My wish has been to blend with the beauty of tropical nature, the moral beauty of a small society. I have also tried to illustrate certain basic truths, one of these being that our happiness consists in living conformably to nature and virtue. I did not have, however, to invent a romance for the purpose of depicting some happy families. I can assert that those about whom I propose to write have really existed and that their story is essentially true. This has been attested to me by several settlers whom I have known

PAUL AND VIRGINIA

on the Isle de France. I have added but a few unimportant details which, coming from my personal experience, only add to its reality. Having some years ago, drawn up a sketch, although most imperfect, of this sort of a pastoral tale, I invited a lady of rank who kept company with the highest society and some grave gentlemen who lived away from it to listen to its reading, as I wished to discover the effect it would produce on readers with such different backgrounds; and I had the satisfaction of seeing them all shed tears. This was the only judgment I could obtain, and it was also all that I wished to know.

But, as grave faults often follow in the train of humble talent, this success inspired me with the vanity of naming my work Tableau de la Nature. *Fortunately, I remembered to what extent the nature of the very climate where I was born was foreign to me; how rich, varied, amiable, luxuriant, mysterious, that of the countries where I have only seen its manifestations as a traveller, and how destitute I am of shrewdness, taste and means of expression, to comprehend and paint it. I then reconsidered my decision and included this feeble essay under the name of, and as a sequel to, my* Etudes de la Nature, *which the public received with so much forbearance, hoping that this title, recalling to their mind my inadequacy, should serve as a constant reminder of their indulgence.*

BERNARDIN DE ST. PIERRE

PAUL AND VIRGINIE

On the eastern slope of the mountain which rises behind Port Louis of the *Isle de France* one can see, on ground which was once cultivated, the remains of two small cottages. They are situated almost in the centre of a small valley formed by large rocks which leave only one opening, and this facing north. On the left can be seen a mountain called *Le Morne de la Découverte*, from which all ships approaching the island are signalled in; and, at the foot of this mountain, lies the town called Port Louis. On the right, one can see the road leading from Port Louis to the District of Pamplemousses; then the church of the same name, which raises its head among alleys of bamboo in the centre of a vast plain; and, further away, forests extending to the extreme limits of the island.

Straight ahead, on the coast, *Baie du Tombeau* is discernible; slightly to the right is the *Cap Malheureux*, and beyond are the high seas where, between wind and water, lie some desert islets, one of which is the *Coin de Mire*, which resembles a bastion rising from the sea.

At the entrance to this valley, from which so many

objects come into view, the mountains re-echo the noise of the winds that stir the neighbouring forests, and the roar of the waves which, in the distance, crash on the reefs; but at the very foot of the cottages, all clamour dies, and nothing meets the eye but huge rocks as steep as walls. Clusters of trees grow at their base, in their crevices and even on their summits where clouds accumulate. Showers of rain, which their peaks attract, often paint the colours of the rainbow on their green and brown flanks and, at their foot, feed the sources from which the little *Rivière des Lataniers* arises. A stony silence reigns in their enclosure, where all is peaceful: the air, the waters and the light. Faintly does the echo repeat the murmur of the palm trees that grow on their high plateaux, and whose tall arrowed leaves can be seen for ever swinging in the wind. Soft is the light at the bottom of this valley where the sun only shines at noontide; but, from break of day, its rays crown the peaks which rise above the shadows of the mountain, assuming gold and purple hues against the azure sky.

I loved to repair to this spot whose wide expanse the traveller may view in peaceful solitude. One day, as I was seated at the foot of these cottages, contemplating the ruins, a man happened to pass by, who was already advanced in years. He wore, according to the fashion of those who dwelt on the plantations, **a short jacket and long trousers.** He walked barefoot, leaning on a staff of ebony. His hair was white, his countenance noble and unassuming. I greeted him with respect. He returned my salutation, and, after considering me for a moment, drew near and came to sit on the mound where I was seated. Encouraged by this sign of confidence, I addressed him. "Father", I said, "could you tell me to whom these two huts formerly belonged ?" "Son", he said, "these hovels and this waste were inhabited, some "twenty years ago, by two families who had found "happiness here. Their story is a touching one; "but in this isle, lying on the route to India, who "is the European who can take an interest in the "fate of some obscure individuals ? Who is he who "would like to live here, albeit happy, but poor "and unknown ? All that men want to know is the "history of great men and kings, and this is of no "use to anybody". "Father", I rejoined, "from your "expression and your speech, it is easy to discern "that you have acquired vast experience. If you "can spare the time, would you please tell me what "you know of the former inhabitants of this waste "and be assured that a man, be he the most tainted "with world prejudice, loves to hear of the happiness "derived from nature and virtue". Then, pressing his hands on his forehead for a while, as one who tries to recollect details, the old man told me the following story :

In the year 1726, a young man from Normandy,

whose name was M. de La Tour, after trying in vain to obtain a commission in the French army and assistance from his relatives, decided to come over to this island to try his fortune. He was accompanied by a young woman whom he dearly loved, and by whom he was loved as tenderly. She was descended from an ancient and wealthy family of his province, but he had married her in secret and she had brought him no dowry, for her parents had opposed their marriage on the ground that he was not of noble birth. He left her at Port Louis, in this island, and embarked for Madagascar, where he hoped to acquire some slaves and promptly return to start a plantation here. He landed in Madagascar, in the unhealthy season, which begins about the middle of October, and, a few days later, died of the pestilential fever which prevails for six months in the year and will for ever prevent Europeans from permanently settling there. Such property as he had taken with him was dispersed after his death, as is usually the case for those who die far from their home. His wife, who had stayed behind in the *Isle de France*, and was then pregnant, found herself a widow; all she possessed in the world was a female slave and that, in a country where she had neither credit nor references. She was determined not to seek assistance from any man after the death of the one man that she had loved, adversity having brought her fortitude. She decided to cultivate, with the help of her slave, a small piece of land, which would provide her with a means of subsistence.

In this almost desert island where any land was free to all comers, she did not select the most fertile regions nor those which were most favourable for trade; but, looking for some mountain gorge, some hidden nook where she could live alone and unknown, she made her way from town towards these rocks where she retired as if to a nest. From some sort of common instinct, all sensitive or suffering creatures seek refuge in the wildest or most deserted spots, as if rocky crags were a defence against misfortune, and as if nature's serenity could appease the turmoils of a miserable soul. But Providence, which brings deliverance to those who are satisfied with the bare necessaries, had a favour in store for Madame de La Tour which neither riches nor magnificence can provide, and this was : a friend.

In that same spot, for the past year, a woman had been living, spirited, kind and sensitive; her name was Marguerite. She was born in Brittany, in a humble family of peasants who adored her and who would certainly have made her happy, had she not chosen, through weakness, to add faith to the protestations of love of a nobleman of her neighbourhood who had sworn to marry her. But, after satisfying his lust, he had abandoned her and even refused to provide her with the means of bringing up a child that she was then expecting by him. She had, therefore, decided to leave for ever her native village and to conceal her misconduct in the colonies, far from her native land where she had lost the one dowry that a poor and honest girl possesses : her reputation. An old slave, bought for a paltry sum which she had borrowed, cultivated with her a small parcel of this district.

Madame de La Tour, accompanied by her female servant, found in this place Marguerite who was nursing her child. She was delighted to meet another woman in a situation which, she thought, was similar to her own. She told her briefly of her past condition and of her present needs. On hearing the story of Madame de La Tour, Marguerite was moved with compassion; and, preferring to deserve her confidence rather than her esteem, she confessed, in all sincerity, the imprudence of which she had been guilty. "As "for me", she said, "I have deserved my fate, but you, "Madame, virtuous and yet unhappy !" and, with tears in her eyes, she offered her both her hut and her friendship. Madame de La Tour, touched by such a tender welcome, pressed her in her arms and exclaimed : "Ah ! God means to put an end to "my affliction, who has inspired in you more kindness "towards me, a stranger, than I have ever found "in my own relatives".

I knew Marguerite and, although I dwell a league and a half from here in the woods, beyond *Montagne Longue*, I considered myself as her neighbour. In a European city, a street, a mere wall, keeps members of the same family from meeting for years, but, in the newly established colonies, we consider as our neighbours those from whom we are only separated by woods and mountains. In those days, especially, when there was little trade between this island and India, the mere fact of being a neighbour established a claim to friendship, and hospitality towards strangers was both a duty and a pleasure. When I came to know that my neighbour had made a friend, I went to see her to try and be of service to them both. In Madame de La Tour, I found a person with an attractive countenance, full of dignity and melancholy. She was then at the last stage of pregnancy. I told these two ladies that, in the interest of their children, and, more especially, to prevent some newcomer from settling there, they should divide between them the lower part of this valley which covered some twenty arpents. They entrusted me with the apportionment and I divided it into two approximately equal portions. One of these comprised the upper part of the valley, extending from the rocky cloud -capped peak, from which *Rivière des Lataniers* takes its source, to the steep opening known as the *Embrasure*, because it resembles a crenel. The foundation of this soil is so full of rocks and gullies that walking over it is hardly possible, and, yet, it produces tall trees and abounds in fountains and rivulets. In the other portion, I included the lower stretch of the circuit, which extends along *Rivière des Lataniers*, as far as this very opening where we are now, whence this river flows to the sea between two hills. You may see here the edge of some meadows and some fairly level ground, but this portion is hardly better than the first; because, in the rainy season, it becomes a swamp, and, in the dry period, it is as hard as lead. To dig a trench, one must cut the soil with an axe. When I had divided the land into two portions, I invited the ladies to draw lots. The higher portion fell to Madame de La Tour and the lower, to Marguerite. They were satisfied with their respective lots, but they requested me not to place their cottages far apart, "so that "we may always", they said, "visit, speak to and "help each other." They, however, needed separate retreats. Marguerite's cottage was in the centre of the valley, just on the border of her estate. I, therefore, built another cottage, close to it, on Madame de La Tour's portion, so that, while close to each other, the two friends were at the same time living on their respective estates. I personally cut paling wood in the mountain and brought latanier leaves from the coast to build these two cottages, whose doors and roof, as you can see, are now gone. Alas ! there is still too much of it left for my memory. Time, which so readily destroys the monuments of kings, seems to spare, in these deserts, those erected to friendship, as if to perpetuate my regrets to the last of my days.

No sooner had the second hut been built than Madame de La Tour gave birth to a girl. I had been godfather to Marguerite's boy whose name was Paul. Madame de La Tour also invited me to act, jointly with her friend, as sponsor for her daughter. The latter gave her the name of Virginie. "She will be virtuous", she said, "and she will be "happy. I only became unhappy when I strayed "from the path of virtue".

By the time Madame de La Tour recovered from her confinement, these two small tenements had begun to bear some fruit, thanks perhaps to the care I bestowed on them occasionally, but, to a much greater degree, to the assiduous work of their slaves. Marguerite's slave, Domingue, belonged to the Iolof tribe; he was still robust, although advancing in years. He had experience and native common sense. He would cultivate indifferently, on either estate, the lands which he thought most fertile and would sow the seed which were most appropriate. He would sow millet and maize in the poorer ground, a little wheat in the best parts, rice in marshy ground, and just below the rocky parts, calabash, pumpkin or cucumber, which love to climb. In the dry land, he would cultivate sweet potatoes, which grow particularly sweet in dry soil, cotton trees on the higher ground, sugar cane on the rich land, coffee on the hills, where the bean is small but excellent; along the river banks and around the cottages, banana trees which, all the year round, bear long clusters of fruit and provide plentiful shade, and, finally, some tobacco with which to dispel his cares and those of his kind mistresses. He used to go and fetch firewood up in the mountain and hew stones, here and there to level the paths. Inspired by his devotion, he carried out all these tasks with intelligence and zeal.

He was deeply attached to Marguerite and hardly less to Madame de La Tour, whose slave he had married at the time when Virginie was born. He deeply loved his wife, Marie. She had been born in Madagascar, where she had learned some crafts, especially that of making baskets and a material called pagne or loin cloth from weeds which grow in the woods. She prepared the food, reared some chicken and would, from time to time, go to Port Louis, where she would sell whatever excess produce there was from these two estates, and this was far from considerable. Add to this, two goats, which were brought up along with the children, and a big dog, which kept night watch outside, and you will have an idea of all the income and household of these two small farms.

As for the two lady friends, they would spin cotton yarn from morning to evening. This work sufficed to provide for their needs and those of their families; but, in fact, they were so lacking in imported articles that they walked barefoot about their estates and only wore shoes when, early on Sunday mornings, they attended mass in the church of Pamplemousses, which you can see there in the distance. This church was further away than was Port Louis, but they seldom went to town, as they were afraid of being treated with contempt because they wore clothes made of coarse blue Bengal linen of the type worn by slaves. After all, can public consideration be worth as much as domestic happiness ? If these ladies had to suffer somewhat when they went out, they felt all the happier on returning home. No sooner did Marie and Domingue, from the high ground, catch sight of them coming up along the road to Pamplemousses, than they would rush to the foot of the hill and help them up the slope. In the eyes of their slaves, the ladies could read the joy they felt at seeing them return. They found in their homestead cleanliness and independence, possessions which they owed exclusively to their toil and to their devoted and affectionate servants.

Attached to each other by common wants and by the memory of almost identical misfortunes, they called each other by the tender names of friend, companion and sister; they had but one will and shared the same interests and the same board. They had everything in common. And, if some old flame, brighter than that of friendship, were to burn within them, pure religious feelings, assisted by habits of chastity, would draw them towards another life, like a flame which rises towards heaven when it has nothing left on earth to live on.

The duties imposed by nature enhanced the happiness of their companionship. Their mutual friendship was intensified by the sight of their children, born of an equally unfortunate love. They took delight in bathing them together in the same bath, putting them to sleep in the same cradle. Each would often suckle the other's baby. "My friend", Madame de la Tour would say, "in this way, each of us will "have two children, and each of our children will "have two mothers". Just as two shoots, left on trees of the same species, after a storm has destroyed all their branches, are likely to produce fruit of richer flavour if each, detached from its native stock, is grafted on its neighbour, so these two children, deprived of all relatives, were developing sentiments more tender than those of son and daughter, or of brother and sister, as they were being fed equally at the breast of the two friends who had given them birth. Their mothers already, over their cradles, were speaking of their marrying each other and this prospect of conjugal bliss with which they beguiled their own sorrows, would often bring tears into their eyes; one would remember that her grief came from having failed to insist on marriage, the other from having submitted to its laws; one for having risen above her status, the other for having fallen from hers. But they took comfort in imagining that, some day, their children, more fortunate than their parents, would, away from the cruel prejudices of Europe, enjoy the pleasures of love and the charm of equality.

In fact, nothing could compare with the attachment which they already displayed for each other. If Paul happened to complain, Virginie was shown to him and, at the sight of her, he would smile and be appeased If Virginie suffered, Paul's cries would soon reveal her suffering, but this lovable girl would immediately conceal her pain to prevent him from suffering for her sake. I hardly ever came here without finding them quite naked, according to the local custom, toddling about, holding each other by the hand and under the arms, as the Gemini are usually depicted. Night itself did not keep them apart, but would often find them resting in the same cradle, cheek to cheek, and breast against breast, their hands round each other's neck, and asleep in a mutual embrace.

When they began to talk, the first names which they learned to give each other were those of brother and sister. Childhood, which knows more tender caresses, knows of no sweeter names. Their friendship increased with the education they received and which led them towards their respective wants. Before long, everything concerned with household management, cleanliness, and the preparation of a rustic meal were within Virginie's province, and her efforts were invariably followed by praises and kisses from her brother. As for him, ever on the move, he would dig the ground with Domingue, or follow him into the woods, carrying a small hatchet; and if, in the course of these excursions, he hit upon some beautiful flower or some fine fruit or a bird's nest, even if these were on the top of a tree, he would climb up and bring them to his sister. Whoever came across one of them, could be sure that the other was not far.

I was coming down one day from the top of that hill when, at the far end of the garden, I saw Virginie running towards the house, covering her head with her petticoat which she had pulled up from behind to protect herself from a heavy shower of rain.

From a distance, I thought she was alone, but, on drawing closer to her to help her walk, I could see that she was holding Paul by the arm, almost completely enveloped in the same covering, laughing merrily at finding themselves sheltering under an umbrella of their own invention. These two charming young faces concealed underneath this bulging petticoat reminded me of Leda's children confined within the same shell.

All they cared to learn was how to please and assist each other. Otherwise, they were as ignorant as natives and could neither read nor write. They did not care to know what had occurred in times gone by and far from them; their curiosity did not extend beyond this mountain. They believed that the limits of the world were those of their own island; and did not imagine that there could be anything worth loving where they themselves were not. Their mutual affection and their love for their mothers claimed the undivided activity of their souls. Never had the learning of useless sciences brought tears into their eyes, nor had lessons of stern morality ever wearied them. That one must not steal they did not know, because everything, between them, was in common; nor be intemperate, because they had simple meals in abundance; nor untruthful, because they had no truth to conceal. Nobody had ever frightened them by saying that God had terrible chastisements in store for ungrateful children; filial affection had been born in them from maternal love. Of religion, they had only been taught what makes it lovable and, although they did not offer long prayers in church, yet, wherever they were, in the fields, or in the woods, they would raise to heaven their innocent hands, and a heart full of filial love.

Thus passed their childhood, as a dawn heralding the brightest of days. They already shared with their mothers all the cares of the household. As soon as the crowing of the cock announced the approach of dawn, Virginie arose, went to fetch water from the neighbouring spring, and returned to the house to prepare breakfast. Soon after, when sunshine crowned the surrounding peaks with gold, Marguerite and her son used to go to the house of Madame de La Tour : they all joined in a prayer, which was followed by the first meal of the day; they often had it sitting on the grass in front of the door, under the cover of banana trees which supplied them with ready-made meals of fruit, and wide, long and glossy leaves which they used as table linen. Wholesome and abundant food was rapidly developing the bodies of these two youths and a gentle education was imparting to their features the purity and contentment of their souls. Virginie was only twelve, and, yet, she already had a shaping waist, long blond hair shaded her face; her blue eyes and coral lips sparkled with the brightest lustre over the freshness of her countenance and they invariably smiled in unison when she spoke; when she was silent, their natural tendency to slant heavenwards gave them an expression of extreme sensibility and even one of slight melancholy. As for Paul, one could already discern in him a manly disposition appearing through the gracefulness of adolescence. He was taller than Virginie, his complexion darker, his nose more aquiline, and his eyes, which were dark, would have had a touch of haughtiness had it not been for the long eyelashes which, like beaming rays, gave them an expression of extreme kindness. Always on the move when alone, he would calm down when his sister appeared, and go and sit next to her.

They sometimes had a whole meal without a word passing between them. By their silence, the simpicity of their attitudes, and the grace of their feet, one could have mistaken them for antique figures carved in white marble representing some of the children of Niobe; but, by their eyes which constantly sought each other, by their smiles which were returned by yet broader smiles, one would have thought they were some heavenly children, two of those blessed children whose nature consists in loving one another, and who need no thoughts or words to express their feelings or friendship.

Madame de La Tour, however, seeing her daughter develop with such an abundance of charm, felt her anxiety increase with her affection. She sometimes said to me : "If I happened to die, what would "become of Virginie, without any means of her "own" ?

She had an aunt in France, a lady of high rank, rich, old and devout, who had so harshly denied her any assistance when she had married M. de La Tour, that she had resolved never to have recourse to her, no matter to what depth of misery she might sink. But now that she was a mother, she no longer feared the humiliation of a refusal. She informed her of the unexpected death of her husband, of the birth of her daughter, and of the difficult situation in which she found herself, devoid of support and with a child to provide for. She received no reply. Although of a proud disposition, she was no longer afraid of being humiliated and of exposing herself to the rebuke of her relative, who had never forgiven her for marrying a man of humble birth, although virtuous. She kept writing to her, whenever opportunity arose, to excite her compassion for Virginie. But many years had gone by without her receiving the slightest manifestation of her remembrance.

At last, in 1738, three years after the arrival of M. de La Bourdonnaye in the island, Madame de La Tour learnt that the Governor wished to deliver to her a letter from her aunt. She hastened to Port Louis, indifferent on this occasion to showing herself there poorly dressed, maternal joy placing her beyond concern for public opinion; and, in fact, M. de La Bourdonnaye did deliver to her a letter from her aunt. The latter stated therein that her niece had deserved her fate for having married an adventurer, a dissolute young man; that passions brought with them their punishment; that her husband's premature death was a divine and just chastisement; that she had been well advised to travel to the islands rather than disgrace her family, in France; that she was, after all, in a pleasant country where everybody, save the lazy, made a fortune. After blaming her niece in these terms, she ended by showering praise on herself : to avoid, so she wrote, the consequences of marriage, which are sometimes disastrous, she had always declined to marry. The truth is, that being ambitious, she was determined to marry none but a man of high rank; but in spite of her riches and although at court the one and only consideration is wealth, none was ever found willing to marry so ill-favoured and hard-hearted a woman.

She added in a post-script that, all things considered, she had warmly recommended her to M. de La Bourdonnaye. She had in fact recommended her, but according to a practice quite common nowadays — which renders a protector more dangerous than a declared enemy : in order to justify, in the eyes of the Governor, her harshness for her niece, she had slandered her while affecting to pity her. Madame de La Tour, whom no unbiased man could have seen without feeling interest and respect for her, was received with extreme coldness by M. de La Bourdonnaye, who was already prejudiced against her. To the account that she gave of her own and her daughter's situation, he only replied in curt and evasive terms : "I shall see..., we shall see..., in the course of "time..., there are so many unfortunate people... "why did you offend a respectable aunt ?... You "are the one who deserves the blame".

Madame de La Tour returned to the plantation bitterly disappointed and broken hearted. She sank into a chair, threw her aunt's letter on the table, and, on entering the house, exclaimed to her friend :

"Here is the result of eleven years of patience !" and, as Madame de La Tour was the only person of all those assembled who could read, she read it out to the family gathering. She had no sooner done than Marguerite remarked with some hastiness : "What need have we of your relatives ? Has God "forsaken us ? He is our sole father. Have we not "lived happy to this day ? Why should you feel "depressed ? You lack fortitude". Seeing Madame de La Tour crying, she threw her arms round her neck, and, hugging her, she exclaimed : "Dear, "dear friend !" But her own sobs choked her voice. At this sight, Virginie burst into tears, pressing alternatively her mother's hands and Marguerite's against her lips and against her heart; and Paul, his eyes ablaze with anger, cried aloud, clenched his fists and stamped his feet, not knowing whom to blame. On hearing so much noise, Domingue and Marie came running and the cottage resounded with cries of grief such as : "Ah ! Madame... my "kind mistress ! my mother !... Don't cry !" Such tokens of affection dispelled Madame de La Tour's sorrow.

She clasped Paul and Virginie in her arms and exclaimed with an expression of contentment : "My children, you are the cause of my affliction, "but you are all my joy. Oh ! dear children ! mis- "fortune has only come to me from afar, but here, "happiness is everywhere around me". Paul and

Virginie did not understand what she meant, but, when they saw her appeased, they smiled and started fondling her.

Thus, happiness was restored, and this scene was but a passing storm in the course of a bright season.

The kindly disposition of these children was growing from day to day. At dawn, on a Sunday, while their mothers were attending early mass in Pamplemousses church, a runaway slave appeared under the banana trees which surrounded their hut. She was reduced to a skeleton, and the only piece of garment she was wearing was a fragment of packing cloth, tied round her loins. She threw herself at the feet of Virginie who was then preparing the family meal, and appealed to her, saying : " My young lady, take pity on a poor "fugitive slave : for a month now I have been wander- "ing in these mountains, half-dead with hunger, often "chased by hunters and their dogs. I am running "away from my master, a wealthy planter of Black "River, who has treated me as you can see". While saying so, she pointed to her body furrowed by deep scars left by the whipping that she had endured, and added : "I wanted to go and drown myself, "but as I knew that you lived here, I thought : "since there still are kind masters in this country, "I must not die yet". Deeply moved, Virginie replied: "Dispel your apprehensions, unfortunate creature. "Eat, eat". And she gave her the meal that she had prepared for the family. Within a matter of minutes, the slave devoured it all.

When she saw that her hunger was appeased, Virginie said : "Poor creature ! I feel like going to "your master and begging of him your pardon. "When he sees you, he will be touched with pity. "Will you take me to his place ?" "You are God's "angel", replied the negress, "and I shall follow you "wherever you wish to go". Virginie called her brother, and asked him to accompany her. The runaway slave took them along paths in the thick of the woods, over high mountains, which they climbed with great difficulty, and across wide rivers, which they forded. At last, towards midday, they reached the foot of a bluff on the border of Black River. There they found a well built house, extensive plantations, and a vast number of slaves engaged in all sorts of work. Their master was walking among them, holding a pipe in his mouth and a rod in his hand. He was tall and lean, with an olive complexion, sunken eyes and dark eyebrows which joined each other. With deep emotion, Virginie approached him, holding Paul by the hand, and implored him, for the love of God, to forgive his slave who was standing a few paces behind them. At first, the owner did not take much account of the two children who were poorly dressed; but, when he noticed Virginie's elegant figure, her beautiful blond hair which appeared beneath her blue hood, and when he heard the sweet tone of her voice which quivered, like all her body, as she begged for pardon, he removed his pipe from his mouth, and, raising his rod to heaven, he swore a frightful oath, stating that he granted the slave her pardon not for the love of God, but for the love of her. Virginie immediately beckoned to the slave to come forward near her master; then she ran away followed by Paul. Together they climbed the back of the hill by which they had descended, and, after reaching the top, they sat under a tree, overwhelmed with fatigue, hunger and thirst. They had travelled more than five leagues since dawn, on an empty stomach. Paul then said to Virginie : "Sister, it is now past noon : you are "hungry and thirsty, we shall find no food here; "let us go down the bluff again to the master of the "slave, and ask him for some food". "Oh ! no, my "friend", Virginie replied, "I was too terrified by "him. Remember what mother sometimes says : "the bread of a wicked man fills your mouth with "gravel". "What shall we do then ?" asked Paul; "these trees produce uneatable fruit. There is not "even a tamarind or a lemon with which to refresh "you". "God will take pity on us", replied Virginie, "he hears the prayers of the little birds who ask him "for food". She had hardly pronounced these words when they heard the sound of a spring flowing from a neighbouring rock. They ran towards it and, after slaking their thirst with its waters, which were clearer than crystal, they gathered and ate some cress which was growing on its brink.

Looking on this side and that to see if they could not find something more substantial to eat, Virginie noticed a young palm-tree growing among the trees in the forest. The cabbage-like heart formed on the top of this tree, at the centre of the leaves, is delicate food, but although its stem was no bigger than a human leg, it stood more than sixty feet high. In fact, the wood of that tree is made up of an aggregate of fibre, but its bark is so hard that it drives back the sharpest axes; and Paul did not even have a knife. It then occurred to him to set fire to the foot of the tree. Another difficulty arose: he had no tinder-box and, besides, although this island is covered with rocks, I do not believe one could find a single flint. Necessity, however, breeds inventiveness and the most useful inventions were often due to the most needy of human beings. Paul decided to kindle a fire after the fashion of natives: with a sharp stone, he dug a small hole in a branch of a tree which was quite dry and which he held steady under his feet, then, with the cutting edge of this same stone, he sharpened the end, equally dry, of part of a branch of another species: he then fixed the point of this stick in the hole he had dug in the branch held under his feet; and, swivelling it between his hands, as one would a whip, to bring out the froth from chocolate cream, in next to no time,

he saw smoke and sparks issuing from their point
of contact. He gathered some dry grass and some
twigs and set fire to the foot of the palm-tree which
soon came down with a loud crash. They used the
fire to strip the heart of its long ligneous and prickly
leaves. They both ate part of the heart raw, and
the rest, baked on a smouldering fire, and found
both equally tasty. They enjoyed their frugal meal,
delighted at the memory of the kind deed they had
done that morning: but their joy was arred by
the anxiety with which, they suspected, their long
absence from home must have filled their mothers.
Virginie was constantly harping on this. But Paul,
who felt his strength restored, affirmed that it would
not be long before they had reassured their parents.

After dinner, they found themselves greatly embarrassed, as they now had no guide to take them
back home. Paul, whom nothing could ruffle, told
Virginie: "Our hut lies in the direction of the midday
"sun. We must, therefore, as we did this morning,
"go over this mountain which you see over there,
"with its three peaks. Come, let us proceed, my
"friend". This mountain was called *Les Trois Mamelles*
after the shape which its peaks assume. They,
accordingly, climbed down from the Black River
bluff, along its northern flank, and, after an hour's
journey, they reached the bank of a large river
which obstructed their way. This extensive stretch
of the island, wholly under forests, is so little known,

even to this day, that several of its rivers and mountains have not yet been given a name. The river on the edge of which they stood flows bubbling along over a bed of rocks. The noise of its waters frightened Virginie: she dared not put a foot in it to wade across. Paul then took Virginie in his arms, and, carrying her, made his way over the slippery rocks in the bed of the river, unscared by the roaring noise of the waters. "Do not be afraid", he told her, "I feel strong with you. If that landowner in Black "River had not consented, on your prayer, to pardon "his slave, I would have fought it out with him". "What", asked Virginie, "with such a tall and cruel "man ? To what dangers have I exposed you ! Good "Heavens ! How difficult it is to do a kind deed ! "Nothing but harm is easy to do." When Paul had reached the bank, he wanted to proceed, carrying his sister, and he made bold, thus loaded, to climb *Les Trois Mamelles*, which he saw, half a league away: but his strength soon failed him, and he had to put her down and to take some rest by her side. Virginie then told him : "Brother ! it is getting dark, "you still have some strength left and mine fails me; "leave me here, go home by yourself and set our "mothers' minds at rest". "Oh ! no", Paul replied, "I shall certainly not leave you. If night overtakes "us in the woods, I shall light a fire, I shall bring "down a palm tree, you will eat its heart and, with " its leaves, I shall build an ajoupa for you". After

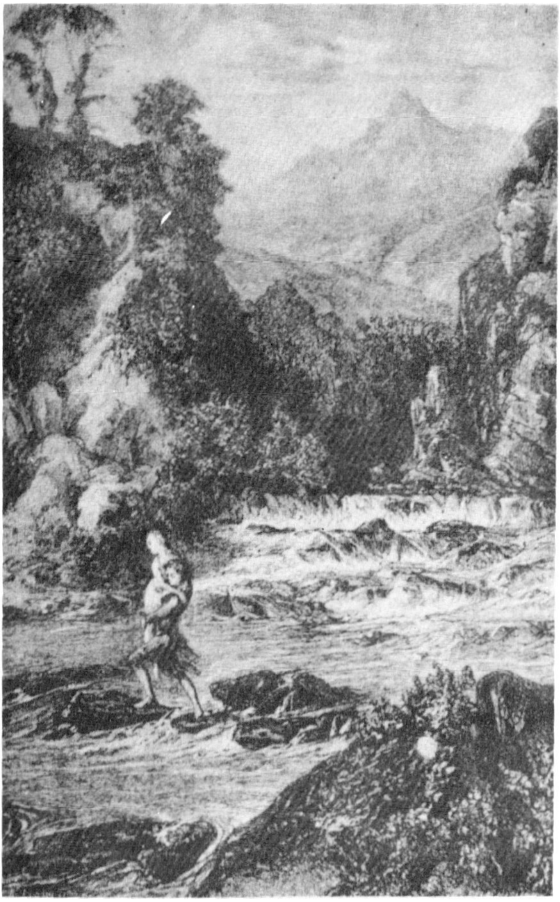

resting for a while, however, Virginie picked from the trunk of an old tree which bent over the bank of the river, some long leaves of hart's tongue which were hanging from its trunk; with these, she made some sort of brodekins and wrapped them round her feet which were bleeding from the injuries caused by the stones along the path: for, in her haste to be of service, she had forgotten to put on her shoes. Feeling relieved by the coolness of these leaves, she pulled off a bamboo stalk and started on her way, resting with one hand on this reed and, with the other, on her brother.

And thus they proceeded slowly through the woods, but the height of the trees and the thickness of their foliage were such that they soon lost sight of *Les Trois Mamelles* mountain, towards which they were directing their steps, and even of the sun which would soon be setting. After a time, they wandered, without noticing it, off the track along which they had hitherto been walking, and found themselves in a maze of trees, creepers and rocks, from which there was no exit. Paul made Virginie sit down, and started running hither and thither, trying to find some way out of the thicket; but he tired himself out in vain. He climbed up a tall tree, in an attempt to discern at least *Les Trois Mamelles* mountain, but he could see nothing around him apart from tree tops, on some of which the last rays of the setting sun were shining. The shadows of the mountains, however, already enveloped the forests in the valleys, the wind was subsiding, as it does when the sun sets; deep silence reigned over these solitudes, and not a sound was audible but the belling of deer looking for shelter in these lonely surroundings.

In the hope that some hunter could hear him, Paul then started shouting at the top of his voice: "Help ! come and help Virginie !". But only the echoes of the forest answered his call, repeating after him, several times : "Virginie !... Virginie!..."

Paul then came down from the tree, overcome by fatigue and by grief; he cast about him for the means of spending the night in this spot: but no fountain was to be found, no palm-tree and not even some branches of dry wood with which to light a fire. Having tried everything, he felt the weakness of his resources, and he started crying. Virginie told him : "Do not cry, my friend, if you do not wish "to afflict me. I am the cause of all your anxieties "and those of our mothers. We should never do "anything, not even a good deed, without consul-"ting our parents. Oh ! how imprudent I have "been !" And tears fell from her eyes. However, she "said to Paul : "Let us pray to God, brother; He "will have mercy on us".

No sooner had they finished praying than they heard the barking of a dog. "This", said Paul, "is "certainly the dog of some hunter who comes at "night to lie in wait for deer". Soon after, the barking of the dog redoubled. "It seems as if this is *Fidèle*, "our own dog", said Virginie. "Oh ! yes, I recognize "his voice. Are we then so near to reaching the foot "of our mountain ?

In fact, a moment later, *Fidèle* was with them, at their feet, barking, groaning and fawning on them. They had not yet recovered from their surprise, when they saw Domingue rushing towards them. At the sight of this kind old negro, who was crying for joy, they started crying too, unable to articulate a single word.

When Domingue had somewhat recovered : "Oh ! "my young masters", he said, "how alarmed your "mothers are ! How shocked when they did not "find you on their return from mass, where I had "accompanied them ! Marie, who was working in "some far corner of the plantation, was unable to "tell us where you had been. I kept going hither and "thither about the plantation, not knowing where "to look for you. At last, I took some old clothes "belonging to both of you, and I caused *Fidèle* "to scent them, and, on the spot, as if the poor thing "had heard me, he set out questing on your trail; "wagging his tail all the while, he took me as far as "Black River. It is there that I learned from a land-"owner that you had taken a fugitive slave back to "him, and that, at your request, he had pardoned "her. And what sort of a pardon ! He showed her "to me, fastened by means of a chain attached to

"her foot, to a log of wood, and with a three-pronged
"iron necklace round her neck. From there, still
"on the scent, *Fidèle* took me to the bluff of Black
"River, where, again, he stopped and barked with
"all his might : that was near a spring where a palm
"tree had been brought down and where a fire was
"still smouldering. Finally, he led me here : we
"are at the foot of *Les Trois Mamelles* mountain
"and full four leagues from home. Come, eat now,
"and restore your strength". And he at once offered
a cake, some fruit and a big calabash, filled with a
beverage made up of water, wine, lemon juice, sugar
and nutmeg, which their mothers had prepared
to brace and refresh them. Virginie sighed at
the thought of the unfortunate runaway slave and
of their mothers' anxiety. Several times she repeated :
"Oh ! how difficult it is to do good". While she
and Paul were refreshing themselves, Domingue lit
a fire and, having looked among the rocks for a
piece of gnarled wood commonly called 'bois de ronde'
which burns although green, emitting a large flame;
he made a torch of it, which he lit, as it was already
night. But he felt much more embarrassed when
the time came for setting out for home. Paul and
Virginie were both unable to walk : their feet were
swollen and red. Domingue wondered whether he
ought to try and find help for them, a long distance
away, or whether he should spend the night with
them on the spot. "Where is the time", he was telling

"them, "when I could carry you both together in my "arms ? You are grown up now, and I have grown "old". He was still thinking the matter over when a group of maroon negroes appeared some twenty paces away. The leader of the group came near Paul and Virginie and said to them: "Kind-hearted children, "you need not be afraid; we saw you going past this "morning, in company with a negress from Black "River; you were going to implore her pardon from "her cruel master; we shall express our gratitude "by carrying you home on our shoulders". On a signal from him, four negroes of the sturdiest immediately made a stretcher with creepers and branches, placed Paul and Virginie on it, and carried them on their shoulders. Domingue was walking ahead of them with his torch, and they all set out amid shouts of joy from the troop who were showering blessings on them. Deeply moved, Virginie said to Paul : "Oh ! my friend, God never allows "a good deed to go unrewarded".

About midnight, they reached the foot of their mountain on whose crest several fires were lit. Hardly had they begun ascending when they could hear voices calling : "Is that you, my children ?" and they and the slaves replied almost in one voice : "Yes, it is...", and, very soon, they could see their mothers and Marie advancing towards them, holding flaming fire-brands. "You naughty children", Madame de La Tour asked, "where are you coming from ? "In what agonies have you thrown us !" and Virginie "replied : "Mother, we are coming from Black River, "where we had been to crave pardon for a poor "runaway slave to whom I had given our breakfast "this morning because she was dying of hunger. "And now some maroon negroes are taking us back". Madame de La Tour embraced her daughter, but she was unable to utter a single word and Virginie, who could feel her face moistened by her mother's tears, exclaimed : "You are compensating me for "all the suffering which I have endured". Marguerite, overwhelmed with joy, was pressing Paul in her arms, saying : "And you too, my boy, have done "a kind deed". When they reached their huts with their children, they gave a copious meal to the maroon negroes, who then returned to their woods after wishing them every sort of happiness.

Every day was a day of happiness and of peace for these families. Neither envy nor ambition ever disturbed them. They had no desire for a vain reputation which is acquired through intrigue, and destroyed by calumny; they were content with being their own witnesses and their own judges. In this island where, as in every European Colony, one is ever eager to collect mischievous anecdotes, their virtues and even their names were unknown. Only, when some passer-by enquired on the road to Pamplemousses from some inhabitants of the plateau:

"Who lives up there in these small cottages ?" they would reply, although they did not know them personally: "They are kind people". In the same way, a violet growing under a bush of thorns exhales its fragrance far and wide, while remaining hidden from the eye. From their conversations they had banished slander, which, while assuming an air of justice, prepares one's heart for hatred or treachery; because one cannot help feeling hatred for those whom one believes to be wicked, nor live with wicked people without concealing one's hatred under the guise of benevolence. And so, slander compels us to live on bad terms with others or with ourselves. But without passing judgment on any individual, they only thought of being charitable to one and all; and, although this was not in their power, they had in their minds a constant determination to do good which filled them with a benevolence always ready to extend outwards. So, although they lived in seclusion, far from being unsociable, they had grown more humane. If the scandals of society did not provide the subject matter of their conversation, the study of nature filled them with ravishment and joy. They admired with ecstasy the generosity of Providence which had made it possible for them to spread among those arid rocks, abundance, beauty, pure and simple pleasures for ever new.

At the age of twelve, Paul, who was sturdier and more clever than European boys of fifteen, had embellished the plantations which Domingue could barely cultivate. He used to accompany him in the neighbouring woods and uproot young plants of lemon, orange, or of tamarind, whose round head is of such a bright green, and date palms, whose fruit is full of a sweet cream which has the flavour of an orange flower. He used to plant these trees, which were already tall, round this compound. He had also sown there some seed of fruit, such as the agathis, with its long clusters of white flowers which hang all round, like the crystal pendants of a chandelier; the Persian lilac, which raises high in the air its flax-grey girandoles; the papaw, whose branchless trunk assumes the shape of a column bristling with green melons, and bears a crown of wide leaves similar to those of the figtree.

He had also planted various kernels, stones of badamiers, mangoes, avocado pears, guavas, jack fruit and jamrose Most of these trees already provided shade and fruit for their young master. His industrious hands had spread fertility even to the most barren corners of this close. Various species of aloes, the prickly pear, covered with yellow flowers spotted with red, the torch thistle raised their heads above the dark crests of the rocks, as if trying to reach the long creepers ablaze with blue and scarlet flowers which hung here and there along the steep slopes of the mountain.

He had arranged his plants in such a manner

that one could enjoy the sight of them at a single glance. In the centre of this valley, he had planted low-growing herbs, then shrubs, then average size trees, and, finally, tall trees which lined the circumference: so that from its centre this vast enclosure looked like an amphitheatre of greenery, fruit and flowers enclosing pot herbs, edges of meadows and fields of rice and corn. But in subjecting these plants to his ground plan, he had not deviated from that of nature. Guided by its indications, he had placed on the higher ground those whose seed are blown about by the wind and, by the water's edge, those whose seed are fashioned for floating. In this way, every plant was growing in the best suited location, and each site received from its plant its natural adornment. The waters which fell from the summit of these rocks formed fountains in some parts of the vale, and, in others, mirrors reflecting the verdure, trees in blossom, the overhanging rocks, and the azure vault of heaven.

In spite of the unevenness of this terrain, most of these plantations were accessible to the hand as well as to the eye; in truth, we all helped him, with our advice and suggestions, to achieve his purpose. He had opened a path round the valley, which, in places, branched off towards the centre from the periphery.

He had used to advantage the most rugged parts and had harmonized in the most pleasant way the ease of a walk with the roughness of the ground, and planted domestic trees among wild varieties. With this vast quantity of rolling stones which, to-day, encumber these roads, and most of the land on this island, he had built pyramids, here and there, in whose foundations, he had introduced some soil and the roots of rose trees, and other shrubs which thrive on rocky ground. In a short time, these dark rough pyramids had been clothed with green vegetation or with the glow of the most beautiful flowers. The ravines, bordered with tall trees sloping over the edges, formed arched cavities protected from the heat, which always afforded some coolness during the day. A path led from a grove of wild trees in the centre of which, sheltered from the wind, some domestic tree was loaded with fruit. On this side, some crop or other, and, on that, an orchard. Through an alley, one could see the houses, through another, the inaccessible heights of the mountain. Under a copse dense with tatamaca trees intertwined with creepers, nothing was visible, even in midday, while on the peak of this large neighbouring rock, projecting from the mountain, everything could be seen which lies within this enclosure, with the sea in the distance, where an occasional ship passed, coming from, or returning to, Europe. On this rock, these families used to assemble in the evening and enjoy in silence the freshness of the air, the fragrance of the flowers, the murmurs of the fountains and the last harmonies of light and shade.

Nothing was more pleasing than the names given to most of the charming retreats of this labyrinth. The rock that I was just referring to, and, from which I could be seen coming from a great distance, was called *La Découverte de l'Amitié*. In their games, Paul and Virginie had fixed a bamboo stalk on it, where a small white handkerchief was raised as soon as they descried my coming, as if to signal my arrival, just as a flag is hoisted on the neighbouring mountain at the sight of a ship at sea. It occurred to me to engrave an inscription on the stem of this reed. However great the pleasure I have derived in the course of my travels from the sight of an antique statue or monument, I enjoy even more reading a finely worded inscription. It then seems to me as if some human voice issued from the stone, making itself heard over the centuries and, addressing itself to man in the wilderness, tells him that he is not alone; that other human beings, in these very places, have felt, thought and suffered as he has; and, if the inscription happens to have been placed by some nation now extinct, then I feel as if it raises our soul into the realms of the infinite, and inspires it with a sense of its immortality, by showing that a thought has survived the downfall of an empire.

I, accordingly, inscribed on the small flagstaff of Paul and Virginie these verses from Horace :

> ...*Fratres Helenae, lucida sidera,*
> *Ventorumque regat pater,*
> *Obstrictis aliis, praeter iapyga**

"May Helen's brothers, charming stars like your-"selves, and may the Father of the winds guide your "course and permit none but the gentle zephyr to "blow".

On the bark of a tatamaca tree, in whose shade Paul would sometimes sit to contemplate, in the distance, the troubled seas, I engraved these verses of Virgil :

> *Fortunatus et ille deos qui novit agrestes !***

"Happy is he, my son, who knoweth none but "the rural deities".

And this other above the entrance door to Madame de La Tour's cottage, where the families usually assembled :

> *At secura quies, et nescia fallere vita.****

> "Here is a conscience which knows no "qualms and a life which knows not deceit".

But Virginie did not approve of my latin; she used to say that my inscription at the foot of her weathercock was too long and too learned. "I should have "preferred this one" she said : "Constantly agitated,

---

* Horace Odes I. 3.
** Virgil Georgics II. l. 493.
*** Virgil Georgics II. l. 467.

"yet constant". "This motto", I replied, "would "suit virtue still better".She blushed at my remark.

These families communicated kindness of heart to everything around them. They had given the most tender names to objects which, in appearance, were most indifferent. A circle of orange, banana and jamrose trees planted round a lawn, in the centre of which Virginie and Paul sometimes danced, was called *Concorde*. An old tree, in whose shade Madame de La Tour and Marguerite had recounted their misfortunes to each other, was called *Les Pleurs Essuyés*. They gave the name of *Bretagne* and *Normandie* to small patches of ground where they had planted corn, strawberries and peas. In imitation of their mistresses, Domingue and Marie, wishing to recall the places of their birth in Africa, gave the names of Angola and Foullepointe to two spots on one of which a particular variety of grass grew from which they made baskets, and the other, where they had planted a calabash tree. In this way, by these productions of their own climes, these families preserved in exile the fond illusions of their native lands, and appeased their yearnings on foreign soil. Alas ! with countless charming names, I have seen come to life the trees, fountains and rocks of this place which has since suffered such convulsion and which, like a field of Greece, has nothing left to offer but ruins and moving names.

But, of all places within this enclosure, none was

more delightful than that which was termed *Le Repos de Virginie*. At the foot of the rock which was *La Découverte de l'Amitié*, is a cavity from which a fountain gushes forth, which, near its source, forms a small pool of water in the centre of a meadow of delicate grass. When Marguerite had given birth to Paul, I had given her an Indian coconut which had been offered to me. She had planted this fruit on the verge of this pool, intending that the tree which would develop therefrom should serve to mark the date of Paul's birth. Following her example, Madame de La Tour had planted another, with the same purpose, when Virginie was born. From these two fruit grew coconut trees, which constituted all the archives of these two families : one was known as Paul's tree, the other as Virginie's. They both grew in the same proportion as their young masters and were somewhat unequal in size, but, after twelve years, had grown taller than their cottages. From their boughs, already intertwined, clusters of young coconut fruit overhung the pool formed by the fountain. Except for the planting of these trees, this cavity had been left adorned as it had been by nature itself. On its dark and humid flanks, large maidenhair ferns radiated forming green and sable stars, and clumps of scolopendras hanging like long ribbons of a purplish green, swayed at the mercy of the winds. Borders of periwinkle grew nearby, whose flowers closely resemble those of the red gillyflower and pimentoes whose blood-red pods are brighter than coral. Some balsam, whose leaves are heartshaped, and some clove-scented basilic, exhaled the most delicious of odours.

From the top of the precipitous slopes of the mountain hung creepers resembling undulating draperies which, on the rocky flanks, formed curtains of greenery. Seabirds, attracted by these peaceful retreats, came and spent the nights there. Towards sunset, one could see curlews and shore larks flitting along the seashore, and, in the ethereal heights, black frigate birds in company with the white bird of the tropics, which, with the star of day, deserted the solitudes of the Indian Ocean. Virginie loved to rest on the border of this fountain decorated with wild and magnificent splendour. She often came to wash the family linen in the shade of the two coconut trees. Sometimes, she took her goats to graze there. While she prepared cheese from their milk, she took pleasure in seeing them browse on maidenhair fern on the steep flanks of the rock, and stand up on the top of a cornice, as on a pedestal. Seeing that this spot was dear to Virginie, Paul brought from the neighbouring forest a variety of bird's nests. The fathers and mothers of these birds followed their brood and settled in this new colony. From time to time, Virginie would scatter grains of rice, maize and millet for them. As soon as she appeared, whistling blackbirds, bengal finches, whose song is so melodious, fodies whose plumage is flame coloured left their bush; parakeets, as green as emeralds, would fly down from the neighbouring latanier palms; partridges flocked round, from under the grass, they all came forward promiscuously, right up to her feet, just like chicken. She and Paul took an extreme delight in watching their pranks, their appetite and their love-making.

Thus lovable children, you passed away your early days in innocence, training yourself in the practice of beneficence ! How often, in this place, have your mothers, pressing you in their arms, thanked Heaven for the consolation that you were preparing to offer them in their old age, and for seeing you advancing in life under such happy auspices ! How often, in the shade of these rocks, have I shared with them your rural meals, which had cost its life to no animal ! Calabashes full of milk, newly laid eggs, cakes of rice presented on banana leaves, basketfuls of sweet potatoes, mangoes, oranges, pomegranates, bananas, custard apples, pineapples, provided at the same time the most wholesome food, the gayest colours, and the most delicious juices.

Their conversation was as gentle and innocent as these repasts. Paul often talked of the day's labours and of the following day's. He was always meditating some scheme for the benefit of their little company. On this side, the paths were by no means smooth;

and, on that, one could not sit in comfort; these young arbours here did not provide sufficient shade: Virginie would be more comfortable there.

During the rainy season, they all spent the day together in the hut, masters and servants alike busy making mats of plaited grass, and bamboo baskets. Arranged alongside the walls, in the most perfect order, one could see rakes, axes and spades; and close to these agricultural implements, the produce whose outcome they were : bags of rice, sheaves of corn, bunches of bananas. Refinement always went hand in hand with affluence. Virginie, taught by Marguerite and by her mother, used to prepare sherbets and cordials from sugar cane, lemon and citron juice.

At nightfall, they had supper by the gleam of a lamp, then Madame de La Tour or Marguerite would tell some stories of travellers somewhere in Europe lost in woods haunted by thieves, or of some ship wrecked by a storm on the coast of some desert island. On hearing these tales, the children's sensitive hearts were incensed and they prayed to heaven that they might some day be granted the favour of showing hospitality to such distressed persons. Then the two families would separate to take their rest, impatient to meet again the following day.

Sometimes, they were lulled to sleep by the noise of a downpour of rain on the roof of their huts, or by that of the winds which brought to their ears the distant murmur of the waves crashing on the shore. They gave thanks to God for their personal safety, the sense of which increased with the thought that danger was remote.

From time to time, Madame de La Tour would read aloud some touching story taken from the Old or the New Testament. They reasoned little over those sacred books; for their theology was mostly one of sentiment, like that of nature, and their ethics those of action, like the Gospel's. They had no days reserved for pleasure and others for melancholy. Every single day was for them one of festivity, and everything around them was a divine temple, in which they incessantly admired an infinite wisdom, all powerful and kindly to man. This feeling of confidence in the supreme power filled them with consolation for the past, courage for the present, and hope for the future. This is how these women, compelled by misfortune to return to nature, had developed in themselves and in their children these sentiments which nature fosters to keep us from falling in adversity.

But as clouds sometimes gather which stir the most equable of tempers, whenever some member of their little company seemed to give way to melancholy, all rallied round him and diverted his mind from thoughts of affliction, more with heart than reason. Each applied his own natural disposition : Marguerite, a lively cheerfulness, Madame de La Tour, a benign theology : Virginie, loving caresses; Paul, his frankness and cordiality; even Marie and Domingue would come to his rescue. They were all afflicted if they saw him afflicted, they cried if they saw him cry. Weak plants, likewise, interlace to withstand the violence of storms.

During the summer months, they attended mass every Sunday in the church of Pamplemousses, whose steeple you can see there in the plain. Some rich estate owners also attended, carried in their palankeens, who sometimes lost no time in meeting these united families, and inviting them to their parties. But they invariably declined these offers, honestly and respectfully, convinced that the rich only court the poor to obtain deference from them, and that one can only be deferent in gratifying someone else's passions, good or bad. On the other hand, they were no less careful to avoid meeting the small owners, generally envious, scandal-mongering and boorish. At first, the former judged them shy and the latter haughty, but their discreet conduct was accompanied by such obliging marks of politeness, especially towards the destitute, that they gradually earned the respect of the rich and the confidence of the poor.

After mass, some kind office was often requested of them. It might be some person in distress who sought their advice, or some child who would ask them to visit its mother who was ill in some neighbouring village. They always brought with them, for the simple complaints of the residents, some useful remedy which they accompanied with that kindness which adds such value to trifling services. They were particularly successful in banishing mental affliction, so intolerable to the lonely or the invalid. Madame de la Tour talked of the Divinity with such confidence that the patient, listening to her, believed in His presence. Virginie frequently returned from these visits her eyes wet with tears, but her heart overflowing with joy, having had an opportunity of doing good.

It was she who, in anticipation, prepared medicines which the patients needed, and who presented them with unutterable grace. After those charity calls, they sometimes went out of their way and passed through the valley of *Montagne Longue*, as far as my house where I was expecting them for dinner on the bank of a little stream which glides nearby. For these occasions, I procured a few bottles of old wine destined to foster the gaiety of our indian repasts by these sweet and heart-warming products of Europe. At other times, we arranged to meet at the sea-side or at the mouth of some other small rivers, which, here, are nothing more than large rivulets. We would bring from the farm some vegetable provisions to which we added those which the sea supplied in abundance. From its shores, we would fish some bull-head, polyps, surmullets, crayfish, prawns, crabs, sea-urchins, oysters, and shell-fish of every description.

In the most terrifying spots we often enjoyed the most peaceful pleasures. Sometimes, seated high on a rock, in the shade of some velvet-leaved Tournefortia we saw the billows from the high seas crashing at our feet with a roar.

Paul, who could swim like a fish, sometimes went out on the reefs to meet their onslaught; and, then, when they drew near, he would run away before the foaming and bellowing eddies which chased him much further up the beach. Virginie would scream at this sight, saying that that sort of a game terrified her.

Our repasts were followed by songs and dances by these two young people. Virginie would sing of the happiness of pastoral life and of the misery of sailors whom stinginess incites to sail on an angry sea, rather than cultivate the land, which supplies such peaceful bounty. Sometimes, after the fashion of negroes, she and Paul would perform a pantomime. Pantomime is the earliest language of man: it is known to all nations and is so natural and expressive that white children will soon learn it when they have seen native children practising it. Virginie, who remembered, among the stories told her by her mother, those by which she had been particularly moved, reproduced their main occurrences with extreme naivety. Sometimes, to the sound of Domingue's tom-tom, she came forward on the lawn, carrying a pitcher on her head, and advanced with timid gait to draw water from a neighbouring fountain. Domingue and Marie, impersonating the shepherds of Madian, would deny access to her and feign to drive her away. Paul would rush to her assistance, beat up the shepherds, fill Virginie's pitcher for her and, placing it on her head, would crown her with a wreath of red-flowered periwinkle, which heightened the whiteness of her skin. Then, joining in their game, I would assume the part of Raguel and give away my daughter Sephora in marriage to Paul.

At some other times, she would impersonate the unfortunate Ruth, returning after a long absence widowed and poor, to her nativeland, where she finds herself a stranger. Domingue and Marie were the reapers. Virginie pretended to glean a few ears of corn on their track, here and there. Paul, with the assumed gravity of a patriarch, questioned her, and she replied, shaking with fear. Ere long, moved with pity, he afforded hospitality to the innocent and a refuge to the unfortunate: he filled Virginie's apron with all sorts of provisions, and brought her before us, as before the ancients of the town, declaring that he was taking her for his wife in spite of her poverty. At the sight of this, Madame de La Tour, remembering her abandonment by her own relatives, her widowhood, then the kind welcome she had received from Marguerite, and elated by the hope of the happy union of their children, could not help crying; and these mixed memories of misfortune and happiness made us all shed tears of sorrow and of joy.

The rendering of these dramas was so perfect that we imagined ourselves transported to the plains of Syria or Palestine. We did not lack the adornments, illuminations and music appropriate to the performance. The stage for the performance was usually set at some crossroads, near a forest whose glades around us formed leafy arches. Seated in the centre, we were protected from the heat during the day but, when the sun had declined on the horizon, its rays intercepted by the trunks of the trees, branched off among the shadows of the forest in long streaks of brilliance which produced the most majestic effect. Sometimes, its entire orb appeared at the extremity of an avenue, and made it sparkle. The leaves of the trees, illuminated from beneath by its saffron rays, shone with the hues of topaz and emerald, their brown and mossy trunks seemed transformed into columns of antique bronze; and the birds, already mute under the leafy bough where they had taken cover for the night, surprised to see a second dawn, all hailed the star of day with countless melodies.

Night frequently overtook us in the course of these pastoral entertainments; but the purity of the air, and the mildness of the climate were such that we could lie down and sleep under an ajoupa

in the midst of the woods, and besides, without
the least apprehension of robbers. On the following
day, we returned to our respective cottages which
we found in the state in which we had left them.
Such were the honesty and simplicity which reigned
in this island not yet opened up to trade, that the
doors of many houses were not secured by means
of a key, and that, for many creoles, a lock was an
object of curiosity.

But there were days in the year which were days
of supreme rejoicing for Paul and Virginie : these
were their mothers' birthdays. Virginie never failed,
the day before, to knead and bake some cakes made
of wheaten flour, which she sent to destitute French
people who had been born on the island and had
never tasted of European bread. Without assistance
from negro servants, they were reduced to feeding
on manioc roots deep in the woods and had, to help
them support their poverty, neither the stupidity
which goes with slavery nor the fortitude which is
acquired with education. These cakes were the only
presents which Virginie could offer from the resources
of the estate; but she offered them with a touch of
extreme kindness which made them of enormous
value. At first, Paul was entrusted with the care of
bringing them to these families, who, on receiving
them, promised to come and spend the following
day with Madame de La Tour and Marguerite.
We could then see a mother coming with two or

PAUL AND VIRGINIE

three daughters, with sallow complexions, emaciated, and so timorous that they dared not lift up their eyes. Virginie would soon make them feel at ease, she would pass round some refreshments, the sweetness of which she heightened by some particular circumstance which, according to her, made it more pleasurable. This beverage had been prepared by Marguerite, that other, by her mother; her brother, for his part, had climbed a tree and picked this fruit right on top. She urged Paul to dance with them. She would not leave them until she saw them happy and contented. She wanted them to share the joy of her family. "One only attains happiness", she used to say "by making others happy". When they left for home, she invited them to take away whatever seemed to have pleased them, disguising the necessity for them of accepting her presents under the pretence of their novelty or uniqueness. If she noticed that their clothes were too shabby, she would select, with her mother's approval, some of her own, and entrust them to Paul to deposit secretly at the door of their huts. In this way, she was being charitable, after the example of the Divinity, by concealing the benefactor and only disclosing the beneficence.

You, Europeans, whose mind, from childhood, is filled with prejudices inconsistent with happiness, cannot imagine that nature can afford such insight and satisfactions. Your soul, confined within a small sphere of human knowledge, soon arrives at the limit of its artificial delights, while nature, like man's heart, is inexhaustible. Paul and Virginie had no clocks, no almanachs, no books of chronology, history or philosophy. The periods of their lives were regulated by those of nature. They knew the hours of the day by the shadows projected by the trees, the seasons by the time they bore their flowers or their fruit; and the years, by the number of harvests. These soothing images added the most powerful charm to their conversations. "It is time for dinner", Virginie would tell the family, "the shadows of the "banana trees are right at my feet" or "night is approa- "ching : the tamarinds fold their leaves". "When "will you come and see us ?" some of her neighbouring friends would enquire, and she would reply: "in "the sugar-cane season" — "Your visit will be all "the more sweet and pleasant", these girls would rejoin. When she was asked her age and that of Paul: "Paul", she would say "has the same age as "the tall coconut tree near the fountain, and, I, that of "the shorter. The mango trees have come into fruit "twelve times and the orange trees have blossomed "twenty four times since I was born". Their life seemed linked to that of the trees, like that of the fauns and dryads. They knew of no historical epochs other than those of their mothers' lives, and no chronology other than that of their orchards, no philosophy other than doing good to everybody and submitting to the will of God.

After all, what need had these youths to be rich and learned after our fashion? Their wants and their ignorance added to their felicity. Not a day passed without their communicating to each other some assistance or some enlightenment; yes, enlightenment; and even if these involved some mistakes, there are none which a man with a pure heart need apprehend. Thus grew those children of nature. No care had wrinkled their brow, no intemperance tainted their blood, no unfortunate passion depraved their heart; love, innocence, piety, day after day, elevated their soul, whose grandeur displayed itself in the unutterable charm of their features, their attitudes and their motions. In the dawn of life, they possessed all its freshness; thus, in the garden of Eden, our first parents appeared, when, coming from the hands of God, they saw and approached each other, conversing as brother and sister: Virginie, like Eve, was sweet, modest and trusting, and Paul, like Adam, allied the stature of a man with the simplicity of a child.

Sometimes, when alone with her (so he himself told me ever so often,) on returning from his labours, he would tell her: "When I am tired, the sight of "you refreshes me. When, high up on the mountain, "I catch sight of you far down in this vale, you "appear to me like a rosebud in the centre of our

"orchards. If you walk towards our mothers' huts,
"your bearing is nobler and your gait lighter than
"that of the partridge running about with its brood.
"Although I may lose sight of you among the trees,
"I need not see you to find you again, for something
"of you which I cannot describe dwells for me in
"the air where you pass, on the grass where you sit.
"Whenever I come near you, all my senses are en-
"tranced. The azure of heaven is not as pure as
"the blue of your eyes nor the song of the bengal
"finch as sweet as the sound of your voice. If I only
"touch you with the tip of my fingers, my whole
"body quivers with delight. Remember the day
"when we went over rolling stones across *Rivière
"des Trois Mamelles*. On reaching the bank, I was
"already extremely tired; but the fact that I was
"carrying you on my back seemed to give me wings
"like a bird's. Tell me, by what spell have you be-
"witched me ? Is it by your wisdom? But our mothers
"are wiser than the two of us. Is it by your caresses?
"But they embrace me more often than you do.
"I believe that it is by your kindness. I shall never
"forget that you once walked barefoot as far as
"*Rivière Noire* to pray for pardon on behalf of a
"poor runaway slave. Come, my beloved, take this
"flowering branch of lemon which I plucked in the
"forest; place it, at night, near your bed. Eat this
"honeycomb: I took it for you from the top of a
"rock. But first, come and rest on my bosom and

"I shall feel refreshed".

"Virginie answered him saying:" Oh! my brother, "the rays of the sun in the morning on the top of "these rocks bring me less joy than does your presence. "I dearly love my own mother and I dearly love yours, "but when they call you their son, I love them even "more tenderly. I am more sensitive to the caresses "they give you than to those I receive from them. "You keep asking me why you love me: but all "beings which have been brought up together love "one another. Look at our birds, brought up in "the same nests, they love one another as we do; "they are always together as we are. Listen how they "call out to one another from tree to tree and how "they answer the call. So, when the echoes convey "to my ears the airs which you play on the flute high "in the mountain, I repeat the words down in the vale. "You have been dear to me, especially from the day "when, for my sake, you wanted to fight the master "of the slave. From that time on, I very often said "to myself; Ah! my brother has a kind heart. But "for him, I should have died of fright. Every day "I pray to God for my mother, for yours, for you "and for our poor servants, but when I pronounce "your name, it seems that my devotion increases. "I keep asking God so earnestly that no harm should "befall you! Why do you go so far or climb so high "to fetch flowers and fruit for me? Have we not "sufficient in our garden? How tired you are! You "are sweating all over". And she wiped his brow and his cheeks with her little white handkerchief and kissed him profusely.

For some time, however, Virginie had been agitated by some unknown emotions. Shadows darkened her bright blue eyes; her complexion was turning sallow, a general langour depressed her whole frame. Serenity had deserted her brow, and smiles, her lips. She would suddenly become gay, without joy, or sad, without grief. She avoided her innocent games, her mild labours, and the company of her beloved family; she would wander in the most secluded parts of the plantation, seeking rest everywhere and finding it nowhere. Sometimes, on seeing Paul, she would advance playfully towards him; then, abruptly, as she was about to accost him, a sudden embarrassment seized her, her pale cheeks turned bright red, and her eyes no longer dared to settle on his. Paul would tell her: "These rocks are clothed with greenness, "our birds sing when they see you, everything around "you is gay, you alone are sad". And he tried to comfort her by his embraces; but she would turn away and run quaking with fear to her mother. The poor child felt disturbed by the caresses of her brother. Paul understood nothing of these new and strange caprices. One ill seldom comes alone.

One of those summers which occasionally spread desolation on the lands lying in the tropical belt, now extended its ravages here. That was towards the end of December, when the sun under the sign of Capricorn, scorches the *Isle de France* for some three weeks with its vertical rays. The southeaster which prevails almost all the year round had ceased to blow. On the roads, strong whirlwinds raised clouds of dust which remained suspended in the air. The earth cracked everywhere; the grass was burnt, warm exhalations emanated from the flank of the mountains, and most of their streams had dried up. No cloud came in from over the sea. During the day, reddish vapours arose from its plains, which, at the setting of the sun, resembled the glow of some fire. Night itself brought no coolness to the smothering atmosphere. The orb of the moon, inordinately large, was rising, all red, on a misty horizon. Herds of cattle, depressed on the hillsides and stretching their necks to heaven, inhaled deeply, and the vale re-echoed with their doleful bellowing. Even their negro herdsman stretched himself on the ground, trying to find coolness; but everywhere the soil was scorched and the stifling air resounded with the humming of insects endeavouring to slake their thirst with the blood of man and beast.

On one of those blazing nights, Virginie felt that all the symptoms of her illness were becoming more severe. She rose, then sat, rested in her bed again, but in no posture could she find sleep or repose. Finally, she finds her way by moonlight to her fountain. There she sees the spring which, in spite of the drought, still flowed in silvery streamlets on the flank of the dark rock. She dips herself in the pond. At first, the coolness revives her senses, and a thousand pleasant memories come back to her mind. She remembers that, when she was a child, her mother and Marguerite took pleasure in bathing her and Paul together in this same spot; that Paul afterwards, reserving this bath for her, had deepened its bed, lined it with sand and sown some fragrant herbs along its borders. On her naked arms and on her bosom she sees the shadows of the two palmtrees which had been planted when she and her brother were born and which, overhead, intertwined their green boughs and their young fruit. She remembers Paul's friendship, sweeter than all perfumes, purer than the water of the fountains, stronger than the interlaced palms, and she sighs. She is conscious of the night and of her solitude and a devouring flame burns in her breast. And then, suddenly, she comes out terrified from those dangerous shades and from waters hotter than the rays of the tropical sun. She runs to her mother, seeking protection against herself. Several times, wishing to tell her of her affliction, she pressed her hands in her own and was on the point of pronouncing the name of Paul; but her oppressed heart left her inarticulate; and, resting her head on her mother's bosom, she could only flood it with her tears.

Madame de La Tour very clearly discerned the

cause of her daughter's complaint but dared not mention it to her. "My child", she said, "turn to God, "who dispenses health and life at His pleasure. He "sends you suffering to-day to reward you to-morrow. "Remember that we are in this world only to practise "virtue".

Meanwhile, these excessive heatwaves raised clouds of vapour from the ocean, which spread over the island like a vast umbrella. They gathered round the mountain tops and long streaks of fire issued occasionally from their misty peaks. Frightening peals of thunder soon re-echoed through the woods, plains and vales; deafening showers of rain fell like cataracts from the skies. Frothy torrents rushed down the flanks of this mountain; the bottom of this basin was turned into a sea, the plateau, where the huts are built, into a small island, and the entrance to this vale into a floodgate from which earth, trees and rocks gushed pell-mell with the roaring waters.

The whole family, shaking with fear, were praying to God, assembled in Madame de La Tour's hut, the roof of which creaked horribly under the stress of the wind. Although the doors and shutters were firmly fastened, every object could be seen distinctly through the joints in the structure, so bright and so frequent were the flashes of lightning. Dauntless, Paul kept going from one hut to the other, followed by Domingue, in spite of the fury of the tempest, fixing a wall here by means of a buttress, driving in a peg there; he only returned to comfort the family with the hope that the weather would soon clear up. In fact, towards nightfall, the rains ceased: the south-east trade-winds resumed their normal course; the thunder clouds were blown towards the north-west, and the setting sun appeared on the horizon.

Virginie's first wish was to see, once again, her resting place. Paul approached her with a bashful look, and offered his arm to help her walk. She accepted it with a smile, and they walked out from the hut. The air was fresh and resonant. Patches of white smoke were rising from the brow of the mountain, streaked here and there with the foam of the drying torrents. As for the garden, it was all scarred by gullies, most of the fruit trees had their roots bared; huge heaps of sand covered the edges of the meadows and had filled up Virginie's bath to the brim. Yet, the two coconut trees were still standing luscious and green but around them nothing was left, no turf, no bowers, no birds, apart from a few bengal finches, which, standing on the crest of the neighbouring rocks, lamented in plaintive notes the loss of their brood.

At the sight of this desolation, Virginie said to Paul: "You had brought birds here, the tempest has "killed them. You had planted this garden, and it "has been destroyed. On this earth, everything "perishes, the Heavens alone do not change!".

Paul replied: "If I could only give you something "from Heaven! but I possess nothing, even on earth". Virginie rejoined with a blush: "You have the portrait "of St. Paul".

She had scarcely spoken these words when Paul ran to fetch it from his mother's hut. This was a miniature of Paul the hermit: Marguerite felt a sincere devotion for it: as a girl, she had long worn it on a chain round her neck; later, when she had become a mother, she had placed it round the neck of her child. It had even happened that, while she was expecting Paul, abandoned by one and all, she had so long contemplated the image of the blessed hermit, that her child had assumed some likeness with it. This had determined her decision to give her son his name, placing him under the patronage of a saint who had spent his life far from all men, one of whom had taken advantage of her and then forsaken her. On receiving this small portrait from the hands of Paul, Virginie, deeply moved, told him: "Brother, this shall never be taken away "from me, as long as I live; and I shall never forget "that you gave me the one and only thing in the "world which you possess". In response to this expression of friendship and this unexpected return to familiarity and affection, Paul attempted to kiss her, but light as a bird, she escaped, leaving him aghast, unable to understand the reason for such an extraordinary behaviour.

Meanwhile, Marguerite was telling Madame de La Tour : Why do we not have our children joined "by marriage ? They have an extreme tenderness for "each other, of which my son is not yet conscious. "When nature will have urged him, vigilance would "be vain; everything is to be feared". Madame de La Tour replied : "They are too young and too poor. "What a sorrow for us if Virginie were to give birth "to unfortunate children whom she may not be "strong enough to bring up ! Your slave "Domingue is worn out with age, Marie is infirm. "I, myself, my dear friend, have grown weak during "the last fifteen years. One ages fast in a hot climate "and faster still in affliction. Paul is our only hope. "Let us wait until age strengthens his constitution, "and until he can support us by his labour".

"At present, as you know, we can hardly satisfy "our daily requirements. But if we were to send "Paul to India for some time, commerce would provide "him with the means of acquiring a slave and, on "his return, we would marry him to Virginie; for I "am convinced that no one could make my dear " daughter so happy as your son Paul would. We " shall talk it over with our neighbour".

In fact, these ladies sought my advice and I shared their views. "The seas around India are calm", I said. "During the favourable season, it is a matter "of six weeks, at most, each way. We shall collect a "few wares for Paul in the neighbourhood, for I have

"neighbours who are very fond of him. Even if we
"gave him nothing but raw cotton, for which we have
"no use, for want of a mill to clean it, some ebony
"wood which is so common here that it is used as
"firewood, and some resin which is wasted in our
"woods : all these fetch a good price in India, but
"are of no use to us here".

I undertook to put in a request to M. de La Bourdonnaye for leave for him to embark on this voyage; but, in the first place, I wanted to inform Paul of it. How great was my astonishment when this young man told me, with more common sense than one would expect from a person of his age. "Why do you
"want me to leave my family for I don't know what
"scheme for making a fortune ? Is there in the world
"a line of trade more profitable than the cultivation
"of a field which sometimes yields fifty or a hundred-
"fold. If we wish to start trading, why can't we do it
"by bringing our excess produce to town without
"my having to travel round India ? Our mothers
"tell me that Domingue is old and worn out, but I
"am young and I grow stronger every day. Suppose
"some accident were to happen to them while I am
"away, and especially to Virginie who is already
"ailing ! Oh ! no, I could not make up my mind to
"leave her".

His answer threw me into serious embarrassment, because Madame de La Tour had not concealed from me the state of mind of Virginie and her own desire to see these two youths mature for a few more years while keeping them apart. These were motives which I did not even dare allow Paul to suspect.

At this juncture, a ship coming from France brought a letter for Madame de La Tour from her aunt. Fear of death, without which the hard-hearted would never be tender, had seized her. She was inviting her niece to return to France, or, if the state of her health did not allow her to undertake such a long voyage, she bade her send Virginie, for whom she would provide an excellent education and a match in princely circles, and to whom she proposed to make a donation of all her property. The return of her kindness, she added, was linked to compliance with her orders.

No sooner read, this letter spread consternation in the family. Domingue and Marie began to cry. Paul, motionless with amazement, seemed about to fly into a passion. Virginie, her eyes fixed on her mother, dared not utter a word. "Could you possibly leave "us now ?" Marguerite asked Madame de la Tour. "No, no, my friend; no, my children", answered "Madame de La Tour, "I shall not leave you. I have "lived among you, and it is among you that I wish "to die. I have only known happiness in your friend- "ship. If my health is unsettled, this is due to past "sorrows. I have been wounded in my heart by the "harshness of my relatives and by the loss of my dear "husband. But, since then, I have enjoyed more

"consolation and felicity with you, in these humble
"huts, than all the riches of my family ever led me to
"hope for in my native land".

At these words, tears of joy flowed from all eyes.
Paul pressing Madame de La Tour in his arms,
said to her : "I shall not leave you either, and I shall
"not travel to India. We shall all work for you,
"dear mother, and you will never lack anything
"while you are with us". Of the whole society, the
one who showed the least joy but who was most
sensitive to these words was Virginie. For the rest
of the day, she displayed a mild cheerfulness, and
her appeasement completely restored the general
satisfaction.

At sunrise, on the next day, when they had just finished the morning prayer which preceded their breakfast, and which they had all offered together, as usual, Domingue informed them that a gentleman on horseback, followed by two slaves, was advancing towards their residence. It was M. de La Bourdonnaye. He entered the hut where the whole family was sitting at table. Virginie had just been serving coffee and boiled rice according to the custom of the country. To these she added hot sweet potatoes and fresh bananas. In lieu of plates and dishes, they only had calabash shells cut into halves, and, for tablecloth, banana leaves. The Governor at first manifested some surprise at the poverty of this **home. Then, addressing Madame de La Tour, he** stated that although public affairs precluded him sometimes from attending to those of individuals, yet she had strong claims to his attention. "You "have in Paris, Madam", he added, "an aunt of "high rank and considerable means who intends to "bequeath her fortune to you and who expects you "to come and live near her".

Madame de La Tour replied that her failing health did not allow her to undertake so long a voyage.

"At least" answered M. de La Bourdonnaye "for the sake of your daughter, so young and so "charming, you could not without injustice, deprive "her of such a large inheritance. I shall not conceal "from you the fact that your aunt has approached "the Government to obtain that she should come to "her. The ministry has written to me officially "on the subject, requesting that I should make use "of my authority if need be : but as I only exercise "this authority for the happiness of the inhabitants "of this colony, I trust that you will readily "sacrifice a few years, as on it depends the "establishment of your daughter and your own "welfare for the rest of your life. Why do people "come out to these islands ? Is it not to try and "make a fortune ? Is it not more agreeable to go "and find it in one's own country ?"

So saying, he laid on the table a large bag of piastres which one of his slaves was carrying. "This" he added **"is intended by your aunt for preparations for the** "voyage of your daughter". He then mildly scolded Madame de La Tour for having failed to appeal to him in her need, while praising, however, her noble courage. Paul, immediately, intervened, and told the Governor : "Sir, my mother did appeal to you "and you gave her a very unpleasant reception". "Have you another child ?" asked M. de La Bourdonnaye from Madame de La Tour. "No, Sir", she replied, "this is the son of my friend, but he and "Virginia belong to us both and are equally dear to us"

"Young man" said the Governor to Paul, "when "you have acquired some experience of the world, "you will understand the misfortune of those in "office, you will know how easy it is to create pre- "judice in their mind, and for them to attribute to "scheming vice what is due to hidden merit".

At Madame de La Tour's invitation, M. de La Bourdonnaye sat next to her at table. He had for breakfast, according to the custom of creoles, a mixture of coffee and rice boiled in water. He was delighted with the orderliness and cleanliness of the little cottage, with the harmony of these two charming families and even with the devotion of their old servants. "All the furniture here is of wood, "but the countenances are serene and the hearts "of gold". Paul, fascinated by the Governor's simplicity, told him : "I wish to be your friend, "because you are a righteous man".

M. de La Bourdonnaye welcomed this mark of

native cordiality. He embraced Paul, shook his hand, and gave him the assurance that he could rely on his friendship.

After breakfast, he took Madame de La Tour apart, and told her that an opportunity would soon offer itself to send her daughter to France on a ship which was ready to sail; that he would recommend her to a lady, a relative of his, who was embarking on this ship : that she would be wise not to give up an immense fortune for the mere satisfaction of a few years. "Your aunt", he added, as he was leaving her, "cannot live more than two years, "I have it from her friends. You should think care- "fully. Fortune does not come our way everyday. "Discuss it among yourselves. All sensible persons "will share my view". She replied that desiring no happiness in the world other than that of her daughter, she would leave the matter of her departure entirely to her inclination.

Madame de La Tour was by no means displeased at this opportunity of separating Virginie and Paul for some time, while providing for their mutual happiness some day. She, therefore, took her daughter aside and said to her : "My child, our servants "are old; Paul is very young : Marguerite is ad- "vancing in years, I am already an invalid; If I "happened to die, what would become of you, "without a fortune, in the midst of these deserts ? **"You would be left all alone, with no one who could**

"be of much assistance to you, and forced, for a living,
"to cultivate the soil ceaselessly, like a hireling.
"This thought grieves me". Virginie answered :
"God has condemned us to work. You have taught
"me to work and to bless him everyday. To this day,
"He has not forsaken us. He will never abandon us.
"His providence takes special care of the ill-starred.
"How often have you told me so, mother ! I could
"not bring myself to leave you". Madame de La
Tour deeply moved, rejoined : "I have no other
"design than to make you happy, and see that some
"day you marry Paul, who is not your brother.
"Think now that it rests with you to make him rich".

A girl who is in love believes that all the world has not noticed it. She places on her eyes the veil that is on her heart; but when this is lifted by a friendly hand, the secret pains of her love escape, as it were, through the open gateway, and the tender effusions of a trusting heart replace the inhibitions and mystery in which she had wrapped herself. Sensitive to these fresh manifestations of kindness from her mother, Virginie related to her how cruel her inward struggle had been, which had had no witness other than God; how she recognized the assistance of His Providence in that of a tender mother who approved of her inclinations and who guided her with her advice; adding that now that she felt strong, thanks to her support, everything induced her to stay with her, without anxiety for the present nor fear for the future.

Seeing that her words, spoken in confidence, had produced an effect contrary to that which she expected, Madame de La Tour told her : "My child, I do not "want to constrain you; make up your mind at "leisure, but you should conceal your love from "Paul. When a girl's heart is won, her lover has no "further request to address to her".

Towards evening, while she was alone with Virginie, a tall man came in, dressed in a blue cassock. He was a clergyman doing missionary work on the island, and Madame de La Tour's and Virginie's confessor. He had been sent by the Governor. "My "children", he said, as he entered, "God be blessed : "you are now rich. You will be in a position to listen "to the promptings of your kind hearts, and give "generously to the poor. I know what M. de La "Bourdonnaye has told you, and what your answer "was. Kind mother, your health compels you to "stay here; but you, young lady, have no excuse. "We must obey Providence and our old parents, "even if they are unjust. It is a sacrifice, but it is an "order from God. He sacrificed his life for us, we must "sacrifice ourselves for the welfare of our family. "Your voyage to France will have a happy ending; "are you not willing to undertake it, my dear young "lady?"

With downcast eyes, Virginie replied in a tremor : "If it is God's command, I shall oppose nothing. "Let God's will be done", she said, all in tears.

The clergyman left and went to apprise the Governor of the success of his mission. In the meantime, Madame de La Tour sent Domingue for me, with a request that I should call at her house, as she wished to consult me regarding Virginie's voyage. I was not at all of the opinion that she should be allowed to go. I hold as an undoubted principle of happiness that we should prefer the advantages of nature to those of wealth, and that we should not seek abroad what we can find at home. These maxims I extend to everything, without any exception. But of what avail could my restraining advice be, when weighed against the illusions of a vast fortune, and my naturalistic motives against worldly prejudices, and an authority which, for Madame de La Tour, was sacred ? This lady only consulted me for the sake of propriety, but her mind was made up from the moment she knew the decision of her confessor. Even Marguerite, who, in spite of the advantages she expected for her son from Virginie's fortune, had firmly opposed the idea of her voyage, ceased raising objections. As for Paul, who was ignorant of the decision which was being made, perplexed by Madame de La Tour's and her daughter's secret conversations, he was abandoning himself to deep despondency. "Some "scheme is being devised against me", he thought, "since I am kept out of it".

Meanwhile, the rumour having spread throughout the island that fortune had visited these crags, we could see traders of every kind journeying hither. Within these poor huts, they displayed the richest stuffs from India, spendid bombasines from Goudelours, kerchiefs from Paliacate and Masulipatan, muslins from Dacca, plain, striped or embroidered, transparent as daylight, baftas from Surat of the purest white, chits of every colour, and of the rarest, with green twig-like stripes on a black background. They unfolded magnificent silks from China, lampas embroidered with open-work, damask linen of a satin white, others of a meadow green, others again dazzling red, pink taffetas, satins in profusion, pekins as soft as woven cloth, white and yellow nankeens and even lambas from Madagascar.

Madame de La Tour wished her daughter to buy everything that would please her, only she was careful of the price and quality of the material, lest the hawkers should deceive her. Virginie selected everything which, she thought would be agreeable to her mother, to Marguerite and her son. "This", she would say "was well-suited for furniture, that for the use of "Marie and Domingue".

Finally, the bag of piastres was spent before she had thought of her own wants. A share had to be made for her from the presents which she had distributed to the company.

Paul, deeply grieved at the sight of these gifts of fortune which foreshadowed Virginie's departure, came to my hut, some days after. Overwhelmed, he said to me : "My sister is going; she is already making "preparations for her voyage. Do please, come to our "house. Use your influence and impress on the mind "of her mother and of mine that they should keep her". I yielded to Paul's entreaties, although convinced that my representations would be of no effect.

If Virginie had appeared to me charming, dressed in blue linen from Bengal with a red kerchief wrapped round her head, she was a far more splendid sight when attired after the fashion of the ladies of this country. She was dressed in white muslin, lined with pink taffeta. Her slim and stately waist outlined perfectly by her bodice, and her blond hair done in double plaits admirably matched her maidenly face. Her beautiful blue eyes were full of melancholy, and her heart, disturbed by a restrained passion, gave a shade of excitement to her complexion, and, to her voice, accents heavy with emotion. The very contrast of her elegant attire, which she seemed to wear unconsciously, rendered her languidness still more touching. No one could see or listen to her without being moved. This increased Paul's melancholy. Marguerite, distressed at her son's state of mind, took him aside and said to him : "Why, my son, "entertain false hopes which make deprivations "still more bitter ? The time has come when I must "disclose to you the secret of your life and of mine. "Mademoiselle de La Tour, by her mother, belongs "to a rich and noble family while you are but the "son of a poor peasant girl and, what is worse, "you are a bastard".

This word 'bastard' caused Paul to wonder. He had never heard it pronounced. He enquired of its meaning from his mother who replied : "You have "had no legitimate father. When I was a maiden, "love drove me to committing a mistake, the fruit "of which you are. My fault has deprived you "of your father's family, and, my repentance, of "your mother's. Unfortunate child, you have no "other relative in the world but me", and she was weeping. Pressing her in his arms, Paul said : "Oh ! "dearest mother ! Since I have no other relative than "you in the world, I shall love you all the more. "But what a secret have you just disclosed to me ! "I can see now the reason which estranged Made- "moiselle de La Tour from me for two months now, "and which determines her to depart. Ah ! no doubt "she feels contempt for me".

Meanwhile, as it was time for supper, we all sat down at table, and each of us agitated by diverse passions, ate little and was silent. Virginie went out first and came to sit at the spot where we are now. Paul soon followed her and came and sat by her side. They both remained silent for a while. It was one of those delightful nights, so frequent in the tropics, the beauty of which the ablest painter would be at a loss to reproduce. The moon was shining in the firmament, surrounded by a curtain of clouds, which its beams dispersed by degrees. Its light was spreading gradually on the mountains of the island and on their peaks which turned silvery green. The winds withheld their breath. We could hear in the woods, at the far corners of the valley, high on the rocks, some feeble cries, the tender murmur of birds playing amorously in their nests, charmed by the splendour of the night and the stillness of the air. Insects themselves, were rustling in the grass. The stars were sparkling in the sky, and were reflected in the sea, which reproduced their flickering image. Virginie, with heedless gaze, was scouring the vast and dark horizon which she could distinguish from the shore of the island, owing to the fires lit by fishermen. At the entrance of the harbour, she noticed a light and a shadow : they were the lantern and the body of the vessel in which she would be embarking for Europe, and which, ready to sail, was waiting at anchor for the end of the calm. At this sight, she lost composure and turned aside so that Paul should not see her cry.

Madame de La Tour, Marguerite and I were seated a few paces away, under the banana trees and, in the silence of the night, we heard their conversation, which I remember distinctly.

Paul said to her : "Mademoiselle, you are leaving "in three days, I am told. Are you not afraid "of exposing yourself to the dangers of the sea... "of the sea that terrifies you so?". "I must obey my "parents and the call of duty", she replied. "You are leaving us" Paul answered, "for a distant relative that you have never seen". "Alas" said Virginie, "I wanted to stay here all my life; my mother did not wish me to. My confessor told me that God's will was that I should go, that life was an ordeal... "Oh ! what a painful ordeal". "What"! Paul rejoined "all these reasons have determined you to go and none has kept you back ! Ah ! there are others which you do not give me. Riches are a powerful allurement. You will soon find, in a new world, someone to whom you will give the name of brother, that you have ceased giving me. This brother you will choose among people worthy of you and enjoying privileges of lineage and wealth which I cannot offer you. But where could you be happier than here ? In what country could you land which would become dearer to you than the one where you were born ? Where will you find a company more lovable than that which loves you ? Will you be able to live without the caresses of your mother to which you are so accustomed ? What will become of herself, who is already aging, when she no longer sees you by her side at table, in the house, or in her walks where she was wont to lean on your arm ? What will become of my mother, who loves you as dearly as your own ? What shall I tell them both, when I see them weeping, lamenting your absence ? Cruel ! I say nothing of me; but

"what will become of me when, in the morning, I
"no longer see you amongst us, and when night falls
"without bringing us together ? When I see these
"two palm-trees planted at the time of our birth and
"which have so long witnessed our mutual friendship?
"Ah ! now that you are called to a new destiny, that
"you are seeking lands other than that of your birth,
"property other than the produce of my work, allow
"me to accompany you on the ship on which you
"embark. I shall reassure you during the storms
"which you so dread on land. I shall rest your head
"on my bosom and I shall warm your heart,
"pressing it against my heart; and, in France, where
"you go to seek wealth and honours, I shall serve
"you as your slave. Happy at the sole idea that you
"are happy, in those mansions where I shall see
"you waited on and adored, I shall still be rich and
"noble enough to offer you the greatest of sacrifices,
"by dying at your feet".

Sobs drowned his voice, and we immediately heard
that of Virginie saying, in words broken by sighs :
"It is for your sake that I am going... for you, whom
"I have seen weighed down by work to feed two
"families of invalids. If I yielded to the opportunity
"of becoming rich, it is to repay you a thousand
"fold the good that you have done us. Is there a for-
"tune worth as much as your friendship ? What
"are you saying concerning your birth ? Ah ! if it
"was still possible for me to take a brother for myself,

"could I choose anyone but you ? Ah ! Paul, to me
"you are far dearer than a brother ! How painful
"it has been for me to keep you away from me !
"I wanted you to help me part with my own self
"until heaven could bless our union. Now, I care not
"whether I stay or I go, I live or I die; do what you
"like with me. Frail girl that I am ! I have been able
"to resist your caresses but I cannot endure your
"anguish".

At these words, Paul seized her in his arms, and holding her tightly clasped, exclaimed in a terrific voice : "I am going with her ! nothing can seperate "me from her". We all ran towards him. Madame de La Tour said to him : "My son, what will become of us "if you leave us ? "

Trembling, he repeated these words : "My son...
"my son !" "You, my mother ! " he said, "It is you
"who are separating the brother from the sister !
"We both sucked your milk; we were brought up
"on your knees, and we have learnt of you to love
"each other; we have confessed it to each other a
"thousand times. And now, you are sending her
"away from me ! You are sending her to Europe,
"to that inhuman country which has denied you a
"shelter, to live with cruel relatives who have rejec-
"ted you. You might tell me : You no longer
"have any right to her : she is not your sister !
"She is everything to me : my wealth, my family,
"my birth, my all. I know of no other now. We have

"shared the same roof, the same cradle, we shall
"share the same grave. If she goes, I must follow her.
"The Governor might prevent me ? Can he prevent
"me from throwing myself into the sea ? I shall
"swim after her. The sea cannot be more fatal to me
"than the land. Unable to live here at her side, I
"shall at least die before her eyes, away from you.
"Inhuman mother ! Pitiless woman ! May these
"billows bring back my corpse to you and rolling it
"up together with hers among the pebbles of these
"shores, afford you, through the loss of both your
"children, an eternal reason for anguish !" On hearing
these words, I seized him in my arms because despair
was robbing him of reason. His eyes flashed fire;
sweat was running profusely down his glowing face,
his knees were shaking, and I could feel his heart
beating furiously in his burning breast.

Virginie, terrified, said to him : "Oh, my friend,
"I call to witness all the pleasures of our tender age,
"your sufferings, my own, and everything which must
"attach one unfortunate creature to another, that
"if I do stay, I shall live for you alone, and if I depart,
"I shall return some day to be your wife. I appeal
"to you all as my witnesses, you who brought me up
"in my childhood, who hold my life in your hands,
"and who behold my tears. I vow by this heaven
"which hears me, by this sea which I must cross,
"by the air which I breathe, and which I have never
"soiled with a lie".

As the sun melts and launches a block of ice down from the summit of the Apennines, so fell this boy's impetuous wrath at the voice of his beloved. His proud head was bent and a flood of tears was streaming from his eyes. His mother, mingling her tears with his, held him in her embrace, unable to utter a word. Madame de La Tour, beside herself, said to me : "I can stand it no further; my soul is "tortured. This wretched voyage will not be accom- "plished. Oh ! my neighbour, please try and take "my son away with you. For the last eight days no "one here has had any sleep".

I said to Paul : "My friend, your sister will not "leave us. To-morrow, we shall speak to the Governor, "let your family rest, and come and stay with me "for the night. It is late, it is midnight, the Southern "Cross is right over the horizon".

He allowed me to take him away without saying a word, and, after a restless night, he arose at break of day and returned home.

But what need is there to relate this story to you any further ? There is only one pleasant side in any human life. Like the globe on which we turn, our rapid revolution only lasts one day, and part of that day cannot receive the light without the other part's being thrown into darkness.

"Father, I beseech you", I told him, "to finish "what you have started telling in such a moving way. "Images of happiness please us, but those of misfor-

"tune teach us. What became of the unfortunate "Paul" ?

The first thing that Paul saw while returning to his residence was Marie, who, high on a rock, was looking towards the high seas. When he first saw her from a distance, he shouted to her : "Where is "Virginie ?" Marie turned her face in the direction of her young master and started weeping. Driven frantic, Paul retraced his steps and ran towards the harbour. There he learnt that Virginie had embarked at daybreak, that her vessel had set sail immediately, and was no longer visible. He returned to the cottage which he crossed without speaking to anybody.

Although this rocky wall behind us looks almost vertical, these green plateaux which make up its total height are like so many floors by which one accedes by steep paths to the base of this slanting and inaccessible cone of rock called *Le Pouce.* At the bottom of this rock is an esplanade covered with tall trees, but so high up and so steep that it resembles a vast forest suspended in mid air, surrounded with awesome precipices. The clouds, which the summit of the *Pouce* constantly attracts around it, feed several rivulets which fall to such a depth at the bottom of the valley which lies at the back of this mountain, that the noise made by their fall is not audible from that height. From that spot, one can see a large part of the island, with its bluffs surmounted by their peaks, amongst which *Pieter Both* and *Les Trois Mamelles*, with their valleys covered with forests; and, further away, the high seas and the island of Bourbon, which lies forty leagues away to the west.

It was from that height that Paul discovered the vessel which was taking Virginie away. He saw it more than ten leagues out at sea, as a black dot in mid ocean. He spent part of the day gazing at it; and, when it had finally disappeared, he imagined that he still saw it; and, when it was lost from view on the misty horizon, he sat down in this wild spot beaten by the winds which incessantly sway the crests of the palms and tatamacas. Their muffled and groaning murmur is like the distant melody of an organ, and inspires a feeling of profound melancholy. It was there that I found Paul, his head resting against the rock, and his eyes fixed upon the ground. I had been following him since dawn : with great difficulty I determined him to come down and return to his family. I led him home and his first impulse on meeting Madame de La Tour was to complain bitterly of the deception she had worked on him.

Madame de La Tour told us that the wind having arisen about three in the morning, and the vessel being about to weigh anchor, the Governor, followed by some members of his staff and by the Missionary, had come to take Virginie in a palankeen, and that, in spite of her own objections, of her tears and of those of Marguerite, everybody shouting that it was for the common good, they had carried her daughter away, almost dying. "At least," said Paul, "if I had bidden "her adieu, I should have been at peace now. I should "have told her : 'Virginie, if during the time that we "have lived together, some word has escaped from "my lips which may have offended you, before leaving "me for ever, tell me that you pardon me for having "said it. I should have told her : Since I am destined "never to see you again, adieu ! my dear Virginie, "adieu ! Live away from me, contented and happy". And, as he saw that his mother and Madame de La Tour were weeping, "Look now for some one "other than me to dry your tears", he said. Then, with a moan, he moved away from them and wandered up and down the plantation. He was roving in all the corners which were particularly dear to Virginie. He was asking her goats and their kids which followed him bleating : "What are you asking me ? You will "never again see in my company the one that used "to feed you from her hand". He went to the spot named *Le repos de Virginie* and, on seeing the birds which fluttered about, he exclaimed : "Poor birds ! "Never again will you greet her who was your kind "fostermother". On seeing *Fidèle* scenting hither and thither and walking ahead of him searching around, he sighed and said : "Ah! you will never again find her." At last, he went and sat on the rock where he had spoken to her the night before, and, at the sight of the sea on which he had seen the vessel disappear which had borne her away, he wept profusely.

During that time, we were following him, step by step, apprehending some tragic sequel to his mental distress. His mother and Madame de La Tour besought him, in the most affectionate terms, not to aggravate their grief by his despair. At last, the latter succeeded in appeasing him by a lavish use of the terms most likely to arouse hope in him. She called him her son, her dear son, her son-in-law, the one for whom she reserved her daughter.

She persuaded him to return home and have some nourishment. He sat down with us at table, next to the place where the companion of his childhood used to sit; and, as if she was still there, he spoke to her and presented her the dishes which he knew pleased her most; but, as soon as he discovered his mistake, he broke into tears. During the ensuing days, he collected every object which she had used, the last bunches of flowers that she had worn, a cup made of the shell of a coconut from which she was wont to drink, and, as if these relics which had belonged to his friend had been the most precious things in the world, he would kiss them and place them on his bosom. The perfume exhaled by amber is not so sweet as the objects which have been touched by the loved one.

At last, perceiving that his grief increased the

two ladies' affliction, and that the wants of the family called for continual work, he applied himself, with the help of Domingue, to restore the garden.

Before long, Paul, hitherto as unconcerned as a native with everything that happens in the world, asked me to teach him how to read and write, to enable him to keep up a correspondence with Virginie. Next, he wanted to learn geography, so that he could form an idea of the country where she would land, and history, so that he should come to learn the ways of the people among whom she would be living. Thus, he had improved his knowledge of agriculture and of the art of laying out gracefully the most irregular piece of ground, thanks to a feeling of love. It is, no doubt, to the delight which this violent and anxious passion inspires that men owe most of the sciences and arts, and it is from its frustrations that philosophy was born, which teaches us to find solace from all pain. In this way, nature having established love as the link between all beings, has made it the prime mover of our society, and the instigator of our intellect and of our pleasures.

Paul did not much relish the study of geography which, instead of describing for us the natural characteristics of each country, only sets out its political divisions. He did not take more interest in history, and especially in modern history in which he found nothing but universal and periodical calamities, whose causes he could not discern; wars waged for no reason and to no purpose, obscure intrigues, nations without character, and heartless rulers. To such reading he preferred that of novels which, dealing in a larger measure with human feelings and interests, sometimes presented situations similar to his own. This is why he enjoyed no other book as much as *Télémaque*, owing to its descriptions of pastoral life and of the natural passions of the human heart. He would read out to his mother and to Madame de La Tour the passages which touched him most deeply; then, moved by some pathetic memories, his voice would falter, and tears would stream from his eyes. He thought he could find in Virginie the dignity and wisdom of Antiope, combined with the misfortunes and the tenderness of Eucharis. On the other hand, he was all upset by the reading of our fashionable novels, full of dissolute morality and principles; and when he came to know that these novels painted a true picture of European society, he feared, not without some semblance of reason, that Virginie might catch its infection and come to forget him.

In fact, over a year had gone by and Madame de La Tour had not heard from her aunt and from her daughter ; but she had learnt from an indirect source, that Virginie had successfully arrived in France. At last, by a vessel which was proceeding to India, she received a parcel and a letter written in Virginie's

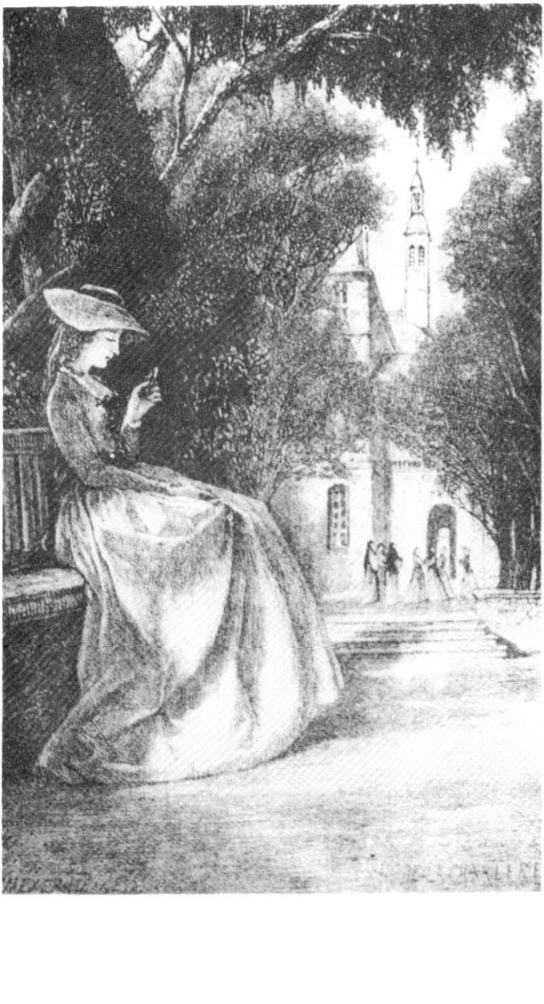

own hand. In spite of the wariness of her kind and forbearing daughter, she formed the opinion that she was most unhappy. The letter described so well her situation and her character that I remember it almost word for word.

"Dearest and beloved mother,
"I have already addressed to you several letters
"written with my own hand, and, as I have never
"received a reply to any of them, I have reason to
"fear that they may not have reached you. I do hope
"that this one fares better, thanks to the measures
"I have taken to send news of me and to hear from
"you.
"I have shed many a tear since the time of our
"parting, I, who had hardly ever wept except over
"the misfortunes of others ! My grand-aunt was
"amazed on my arrival when on being questioned
"as to my accomplishments, I told her that I could
"neither read nor write. She asked what then I had
"learnt since I had been born, and on my replying
"that I had been taught to take care of the household
"and to consult your wishes, she told me that
"I had received the education of a maid servant.
"The next day, she placed me as a boarder in a
"great monastery, near Paris, where I have masters
"of all sorts : they teach me, amongst other things,
"history, geography, grammar, mathematics and
"riding, but I am so poorly gifted for all these sciences,
" that I shall derive little benefit from the teach-

"ing of these masters. I feel a poor creature with
"a weak intellect, as they sometimes hint. My
"aunt's kindnesses however do not relax. She
"gives me new dresses each season. She has placed
"beside me two chamber maids, who are as well
"dressed as ladies of high rank. She had made me
"assume the title of countess, and renounce my
"name of de La Tour, which was as dear to me
"as it is to you, because of all you have told me
"of the misery which my father endured in order
"to marry you. She has replaced your married
"name by that of your family, which is dear
"to me, however, because it was your maiden name.
"Finding myself in such a prosperous situation, I
"besought her to send you some succour. How
"shall I convey to you her reply ? But you have
"recommended that I should always speak the truth.
"So, she replied that some little help would be of
"no use, and that, in the simple life that you were
"leading, a great deal would embarrass you. I first
"sought to send you tidings in a hand other than
"mine, but as I had here, on my arrival, no one in
"whom I could place my trust, I applied myself
"night and day to learn how to read and write:
"God did me the favour of enabling me to do both
"in a short time. I entrusted the care of sending my
"first letters to the ladies who are around me, who, I
"have reason to believe, handed them over to my
"grand-aunt. This time, I have had recourse to a

"boarder friend of mine: it is at her address, herewith
"enclosed, that I request you to send me your
"answers. My grand-aunt had forbidden me to
"entertain any outward correspondence, which could,
"according to her, create an obstacle to the ambi-
"tious designs that she has formed for me. She is the
"only one who can see me at the gate, apart from
"an old nobleman, a friend of hers, who, she says,
"takes a strong fancy to me. To speak the truth,
"I take none whatever to him, even if I ever could
"take a fancy to somebody".

"I live amid the lustre of wealth, and I do not
"dispose of a single cent. I am told that if I had
"money, that would create a wrong impression.
"Even my dresses belong to my parlourmaids who
"contend for their possession before I have laid
"them aside. In the midst of riches, I am very much
"poorer than I was when I lived with you, because
"I have nothing to give away. When I saw that the
"great talents which I was being taught would not
"procure me the possibility of doing the least good,
"I have had recourse to my needle, the use of
"which, fortunately, I had learnt from you. I am
"sending you accordingly several pairs of stockings
"of my own making, for you and mother Margue-
"rite, a cap for Domingue, and one of my red
"kerchiefs for Marie. I am adding to this parcel,
"some pips and stones of the fruit I have had for
"my collations, together with seed of various trees

"which I collected during recreation in the garden
"of the monastery. To these I have also added some
"seed of violets, daisies, crowfoot, poppy, corn-
"flower and scabious plants which I gathered in the
"fields. There are, in the meadows of this country,
"more lovely flowers than in ours, but nobody
"cares for them. I feel sure that mother Marguerite
"and you will derive more pleasure from this bag
"of seed than from the bag of piastres which has
"been the cause of our separation, and of my tears.
"It will be a great joy for me if you have the satis-
"faction some day of seeing apple trees growing side
"by side with our banana trees, and beech trees
"blending their foliage with that of our coconuts.
"You will fancy yourself in that Normandy which
"you so dearly love."

"You have bidden me acquaint you of my joys
"and my sorrows. I have no more joys far from
"you; and, as for my sorrows, I allay them by the
"thought that you have assigned this station to me
"by the will of God. But the deepest sorrow I feel
"comes from the fact that nobody here speaks to
"me of you, and that I cannot speak of you to anyone.
"My parlourmaids, or rather those of my grand-
"aunt, for they are attached to her more than
"to me, tell me, whenever I try to bring the conver-
"sation round to objects which are so dear to me:
"Remember, Mademoiselle, that you are a French
"lady and that you must forget that country of

"savages". Alas ! I would sooner forget myself "than forget the place where I was born and where "you are living ! It is this country which, to me, is "a land of savages, because I live alone, having no "one to whom I could confide the love which shall "bear to her grave,

Very dear and beloved mother,

Your obedient and affectionate daughter,

"*Virginie de La Tour*"

"I commend to your benevolence Marie and "Domingue who bestowed such care on my childhood; "caress Fidèle for me, he who discovered me in the "woods".

Paul was very surprised at the fact that Virginie made no mention of him, she, who had not forgotten in her reminiscences the house dog; but he did not know that, however long a woman's letter, she never expresses her most precious thought before the end.

In a post-script, Virginie specially recommended to Paul two sorts of seed, those of violets and scabious. She gave him some information regarding the nature of these plants and the most suitable places where to sow them. "The violet", she wrote "bears a small "flower of a deep purple, which likes to hide "itself in the bush, where one soon discovers it owing "to its delightful scent".

"She bade him sow it beside the spring, at the foot "of her coconut tree. "Scabious", she added, "bears "a beautiful flower of a very pale blue, dotted white "on a black background. One would think it was in "mourning. For this reason it is also called the widow's "flower. It thrives in rugged and wind-swept tracts". She requested him to sow its seed on the rock where she had spoken to him at night for the last time, and to name this rock, for the love of her, *Le Rocher des Adieux*. She had enclosed the seed in a small purse of very plain material, but which, to Paul, appeared invaluable, when he noticed a P and a V interwoven with hair which he identified, by their beauty, as being those of Virginie.

The letter of this sensitive and virtuous girl caused the whole family to shed tears. Her mother replied to her, in the name of the whole company, that she could stay or return as she pleased, giving her the assurance that they had all lost the best part of their happiness from the moment she had gone and that she, in particular, was disconsolate.

Paul wrote to her a very long letter, in which he assured her that he would make the garden worthy of her, and mix European plants with those of Africa, in the same way as she had interlaced their names in her needlework. He was sending her coconuts from the trees growing near her fountain and which had reached full maturity. He was not adding any other indigenous seeds from their island home, so that the desire to see their produce again might determine her early return. He entreated her to accede to the earnest wish of their family and to his own, in particular, since he could never taste of happiness again if separated from her.

With care, with the utmost care, Paul sowed the European seed, and especially those of violets and scabious, the flowers which seemed to bear some analogy to the character and situation of Virginie, who had recommended them so expressly; but, whether because they had been injured by exposure to the air during the voyage, or rather because the climate of this part of Africa did not suit them, very few of them germinated, and even these failed to thrive.

In the meantime, envy, which pursues the happiness of man, especially in the French colonies, spread rumours throughout the island which caused Paul grave anxiety. Persons on board the vessel which had brought Virginie's letter asserted that she was on the point of getting married ; they even named the nobleman who would marry her ; some of them went the length of asserting that the wedding had already taken place and that they had witnessed it. Paul at first despised the news brought by a trading vessel which often spreads false rumours along its course. But as several inhabitants of the island, through perfidy, hastened to sympathize with him for his misfortune, he began to give it some credit. Besides, in some of the novels which he had read, he had seen breaches of faith treated as the subject of amusement and, as he knew that these books contained fairly true pictures of European morality, he was afraid that Madame de La Tour's daughter might eventually become tainted and might forget her former pledges. The little learning he had acquired made him miserable. What considerably intensified his fears was the fact that several vessels arrived here from Europe during the space of six months without bringing news of Virginia.

The unfortunate young man in the pangs of anxiety often came to see me, to seek from my experience of the world, confirmation or appeasement of his anxieties.

As I told you, I live about a league and a half from here, on the bank of a small river, which flows along the flank of *Montagne Longue*. There I spend my days in loneliness, without wife, children or servants.

Next to the supreme happiness of having found a wellmatched companion, the least unhappy state of life probably is that of a solitary. Every man who has had to suffer at the hands of his fellows aspires to solitude. It is even remarkable that nations which are unhappy because of their opinions, their customs and traditions or their government, have produced classes of citizens entirely devoted to solitude and celibacy. Such were the Egyptians when on their decline, the Greeks of the Byzantine empire, and such, in our day, are the Indians, the Chinese, the modern Greeks, the Italians, and most of the nations of Eastern and

Southern Europe. Solitude leads man back some way towards natural happiness, by removing from him social misfortune. In the midst of our societies, divided by so much prejudice, our soul is in a constant state of restlessness ; it turns over unceasingly countless turbulent and contradictory opinions, with which the members of an ambitious and miserable society seek to subdue one another. But, while in loneliness it sheds these disturbing emotions, it reasserts its identity of nature and of its maker. So the muddy water of a torrent which works havoc in the fields, should it happen to flow into a small pond, away from its course, deposits its slime at the bottom of its bed, and recovers its pristine limpidity, and, having regained its transparency, reflects, together with its own banks, the greenery of the earth and the light of the skies. Solitude restores the harmonies of the body as well as those of the soul. It is among hermits that are to be found the men who drive to its furthest limits the career of life; such are the Brahmins of India. Finally, I believe it to be so necessary, even to worldly happiness that it seems to me impossible for anyone to enjoy any lasting pleasure, whatever one's mood, or to regulate one's conduct according to some established principle, unless one creates, within oneself, a solitude from which one's opinions seldom emerge, and into which those of others never enter. I do not mean to say, however that man should live in absolute loneliness; he is linked to all mankind by his wants; he, therefore, owes his work to his fellow men ; he owes himself also to the rest of nature.

But, as God has given each of us organs perfectly suited to the elements in the midst of which we live, feet to walk on the ground, lungs to breathe the air, eyes to see with, without it being possible for us to interchange the use of these senses, He has reserved for Himself alone, as the source of all life, the heart, which is the most important organ.

I therefore spend my days far from my fellow men whom I wished to serve and who persecuted me. After travelling round a number of countries of Europe, and a few states of America and Africa, I fixed my abode in this thinly populated island, attracted by the seduction of its mild climate and by its solitude. A cottage which I built in the forest at the foot of a tree, a small field cleared with my own hands, a stream which flows past my doorstep, suffice for my wants and my pleasures. To these satisfactions, I add that which I derive from some books from whose ethics I learn to become more virtuous. They even turn that world which I have left, into an instrument of my happiness : they present to me scenes of passions which make its inhabitants so miserable; and by the comparison which I establish between their fate and mine, they cause me to enjoy a negative happiness. Like a man saved from a shipwreck and perched on a rock, I gaze from my loneliness on the storms which shake the rest of the world. : Even my peacefulness is enhanced by the distant clamour of the storm. Ever since men no longer stand in my way, nor I in theirs, I have ceased hating them, I pity them. If I happen to meet some ill-fated person, I endeavour to help him with my advice, as a passer-by, on the bank of a river, holds out a helping hand to a hapless man who is drowning. But I have found none but the innocent to pay heed to my advice. In vain does nature summon to it the rest of humanity : each man forms an image of it which he clothes with his own passions. All his life he pursues this empty shadow which leads him astray, and then he complains to heaven of the mistaken image which he has shaped for himself. Of the large number of ill-starred beings whom I have tried to bring back to nature, I have not found a single one but was engrossed in his own misery. They would listen to me attentively at first, hoping that I would help them acquire glory or wealth; but on discovering that I only meant to teach them how to do without these, they would pity me for not running after their fatal happiness; they would disapprove of my leading a secluded life; they would claim that they alone were useful to mankind, and they would endeavour to drag me in their giddy round. But if I communicate with everybody, I do not give myself away to anyone. Sometimes, it is enough for me that I should take my own self as an example. I recall, in my present serenity, the past tumult of my own life, to which I had once attached such value: favours, riches, fame, luxury and opinions which differ all over the world. I compare so many men whom I have seen contending furiously with one another for these idle fancies, and who now are no more, to the waves of my river which crash, foaming, against the rocks embedded in its course, and disappear never to return. As for me, I allow myself to be led peacefully on the tide of time, towards the ocean of the future which has no bounds; and, assisted by visions of the true harmonies of nature, I elevate my soul towards its Maker, looking forward to happier destinies in another world.

Although from my hermitage in the heart of the forest, the eye cannot see that multitude of objects which the elevation of ground on which we stand presents to view, there are yet to be found attractive arrangements for one who, like me, prefers to retire within himself rather than expand outwardly. The stream that glides past my door flows in a straight line across the woods, and looks like a long canal shaded with trees of all sorts of leafage: there are tatamacas, ebonies, and some which are commonly called here apple wood, olive wood and cinnamon; in places, groves of palmtrees raise their naked pillars more than a hundred feet tall, surmounted with a crown of palms, which appear above the surrounding trees, as if one forest had been planted over another. there are mixed creepers of various sorts, intertwining from tree to tree, which form, in one place, arches of flowers, and, in another, curtains of greenery. Spicy odours are exhaled by most of these trees, and their fragrance adheres so tenaciously to one's clothes that it is possible here to discern a man who has been through a forest, several hours after he has come out of it. In the season when they blossom, you would think they were covered with snow. Towards the end of summer a variety of foreign birds, led by an inscrutable instinct, come from unknown lands beyond the seas, to pick the seed from plants growing on the island, and contrast the brightness of their plumage with the greenness of the trees made a shade darker by the sun. Such, amongst others, are various sorts of parakeets, the blue pigeon, called here the dutch pigeon. Monkeys, denizens of these forests, frolic among the dark boughs, from which they stand out conspicuously with their grey and greenish coat and their black face; some of them hang by their tail and swing in the air, others jump from one branch to another, carrying their young in their arms. Never yet has the murderous gun frightened these peaceful children of nature. You can hear nothing but cries of joy, the unknown twitterings and warblings of some birds from the southern lands, which the echoes of these forests repeat in the distance. The river which flows bubbling by on a bed of rock bordered with trees, reflects here and there in its limpid waters their venerable masses of verdure and of shade, together with the pranks of their happy inhabitants. A thousand paces away, it dashes down successive platforms of rocks, and forms, where it falls, a sheet of water as smooth as crystal which comes down crashing into foam. A thousand confused noises issue from its tumultuous waters, and, scattered by the winds throughout the forest, sometimes, escape far and wide, while, at other times, they all congregate and deafen as would the ringing of cathedral bells. The air, constantly renewed by the motion of the waters, maintains on the banks of this river, in spite of the extremely hot summer, a verdure and a coolness seldom found on this island, even on the summit of its mountains.

Some distance away is a rock far enough from the waterfall to save one from being deafened by the noise of the waters, yet near enough to allow one to enjoy their sight, their coolness and their gentle murmur. Sometimes, in the hot season, Madame de La Tour, Marguerite, Virginie, Paul and I dined in the shade of this rock. Virginie, who always directed even her simplest actions to the welfare of others, never ate a fruit without planting its stone or kernel. "Trees will grow from them", she would say, "which will give their fruit to some traveller, or, at "any rate, to some bird". So, one day, after eating a papaw at the foot of this rock, she planted its seed.

Soon after, there grew several trees, amongst which was a female one, that is, the one which bears the fruit. This tree barely reached up to Virginie's knee when she departed, but, being a fast grower, it had, after two years, reached a height of twenty feet, and the upper portion of its trunk was surrounded by several rows of ripe fruit. Paul, who had accidentally visited this spot, was delighted when he saw that tall tree, risen from a small seed which he had seen planted by his friend; and he immediately sank into a deep melancholy, for it bore witness to her long absence. The sight of the same objects day after day prevents us from noticing how fast our life is spent, they decline with us, unnoticeably; but it is those that we suddenly see again after losing sight of them for some years, which warn us of the swiftness with which the stream of our life is gliding away. Paul was as surprised and as disturbed at the sight of that tall papaw tree loaded with fruit, as is a traveller who, after a long absence from his native land, fails to see his contemporaries, but finds their children who were still at the breast when he left them, and who have since, themselves, become the fathers of families. At one time, he thought of cutting it down, because it recalled too vividly the length of time that had elapsed since the departure of Virginie, and then, considering it as a memorial to her generosity, he kissed its trunk, addressing it with words full of tenderness and regret.

O tree, whose posterity still exists in our woods,

I have looked upon you myself with deeper interest and veneration than upon the triumphal arches of the Romans! May nature, which every day destroys the monuments of royal ambitions, multiply throughout our forests those which we owe to the beneficence of a poor young girl!

It was at the foot of this papaw tree that I was sure to meet Paul when he came into my neighbourhood. One day, I found him there, overwhelmed with melancholy, and we had a conversation which I propose to relate to you, if you do not find me tedious with my long digressions, pardonable considering my age, and the fact that they were my last friends. I shall relate it in the form of a dialogue, to allow you to appreciate the native common sense of this youth and it will be easy for you to distinguish the speakers from each other by the trend of his questions and of my answers. He said to me : "I am "deeply grieved. It is two years and two months "now that Mademoiselle de La Tour has left, and, for "the last eight and a half months, we have not heard "from her. She is rich, and I am poor : she has "forgotten me. I want to board a ship I shall go to "France, I shall serve the king there, I shall make a "fortune and the grand-aunt of Mademoiselle de La "Tour will consent to my marrying her grand-niece "when I shall have become a nobleman".

THE OLD MAN

"Oh, my friend! have you not told me that you
"are not of noble birth ?"

PAUL

"My mother told me so; but as for me, I do not
"know what noble birth means. I have never noticed
"that I had less of it than anyone else, nor that others
"had more than I".

THE OLD MAN

"In France, humble birth closes to you the paths
"leading to high office. There is more : you cannot
"even secure admission to any distinguished guild".

PAUL

"You have told me on several occasions, that one
"of the reasons for the grandeur of France was that
"the most humble subject could accede to everything,
"and you have quoted the names of many famous men
"who, having been born in some modest station,
"have been an honour to their native land. So, you only
"meant to beguile my courage ?"

THE OLD MAN

"My son, I shall never destroy it, I have told you

"the truth concerning the past; but things have changed
"considerably now: everything in France, these days,
"has become venal; everything is the patrimony of a
"small number of families or the property of power-
"ful guilds. The king is like a sun which the nobility
"and various corps surround like clouds, it is hardly
"possible that one of its rays should fall on you.
"Formerly, in a less complicated administration,
"such phenomena have been known to occur. Talent
"and merit then developed on all sides, like virgin
"lands which, happening to be cleared, yield with
"all their strength. But great kings who know how
"to distinguish men from one another, and how
"to choose them, are rare. The average king only
"yields to the impulse of the nobility and of the
"corporations that surrounds them".

PAUL

"But I may, perhaps, find one of these noblemen
"who will protect me?"

THE OLD MAN

"To earn the protection of the powerful, one must
"serve his ambitions and his passions. You will never
"succeed because you have no ancestry and you have
"integrity".

PAUL

"But I shall do such daring deeds, I shall be so
"true to my word, so punctual in the performance
"of my duties, so zealous and so constant in my
"friendship, that I shall deserve adoption by one
"of them, as I have seen it done in the old stories that
"you made me read".

THE OLD MAN

"Oh! my friend! With the Greeks and the Romans,
"even on their decline, the powerful had respect for
"virtue; but we have had numbers of men famous in
"all sorts of ways, born in the lower classes, and yet
"I do not know of any who has been adopted by a
"noble family. Were it not for our kings, virtue in
"France would be doomed to remain eternally
"plebeian. As I told you already, they sometimes
"honour it when they notice it, but the distinctions
"which were formerly reserved for it are now only
"awarded for money".

PAUL

"Failing some powerful protector, I shall try and
"win the favour of some guild. I shall adopt its
"spirit and its opinions; I shall earn its affection.

THE OLD MAN

"And so, you will do like every other man; you will
"sacrifice your conscience in order to attain wealth!"

PAUL

"Oh! no! I shall never seek anything but truth".

THE OLD MAN

"Instead of inspiring affection, you might very well
"inspire hatred. Besides, corporations are very little
"interested in discovering truth. The ambitious are
"indifferent to opinions as long as they rule".

PAUL

"How unfortunate am I! Everything repels me.
"I am doomed to spend my life labouring in obscu-
"rity, far from Virginie!"

And he heaved a deep sigh.

THE OLD MAN

"Let God be your sole patron, and humanity your
"guild, you should be devoted constantly to the one
"and to the other. Families, peoples, kings, have their

"prejudices and their passions : they must often be
"served by vice. God and humanity only expect virtue
"from us".

"But why do you wish to be distinguished from the
"rest of mankind? This is a feeling which is not
"natural, because if every one had it, everyone would
"be at war with his neighbour. Be content to do your
"duty in the station which Providence has assigned to
"you. Bless your destiny which allows you to have
"a conscience of your own, and which does not compel
"you, like the powerful, to ground your happiness
"on the opinion of the humble, and, like the humble,
"to crawl before the powerful for a living. You are in a
"country and a situation where, for your subsistence,
"you need neither deceive, nor flatter, nor degrade your-
"self, as do most of those who seek riches in Europe;
"where your station does not forbid you to practise
"virtue; where you may, with impunity, be kind,
"truthful, sincere, learned, patient, sober, chaste,
"forbearing, pious, without seeing, tarnished by
"ridicule, your wisdom which is still in its prime.
"Heaven has given you freedom, health, a good
"conscience and friends: the kings to whose favour
"you aspire are not as fortunate."

PAUL

"Oh! I do miss Virginie! Without her, I have
"nothing; with her, I would have everything She

"alone is my ancestry, my glory and my fortune.
"But since, after all, her relative wants her to marry
"a man with a great name: with the help of books,
"I shall become learned and famous; I am going to
"study. I shall acquire knowledge; I shall serve my
"native land usefully by my learning, without doing
"harm to any man or being dependent on any.
"I shall acquire fame, and that glory will belong to no
"one but me".

THE OLD MAN

"Son, talents are even rarer than birth and riches,
"and no doubt are more valuable, because nothing
"can take them away and everywhere they earn public
"esteem. But they cost a lot. One only acquires them
"at the expense of privations of all sorts, of an exquisite
"sensitiveness which makes us miserable at home
"and even abroad by reason of the persecutions
"of our contemporaries. A lawyer in France does not
"envy a soldier's fame, nor does a soldier that of a
"sailor; but everyone there will come across your way
"because everyone claims to have knowledge. You
"would serve mankind, so you say? But the man who
"can produce an extra sheaf of corn in a field does a
"greater service to mankind than he who gives it a book".

PAUL

"Oh! she who has planted this papaw tree has

"made a more valuable gift to the inhabitants of
"these forests than if she had given them a library."

With these words, he clasped this tree in his arms
and kissed it with rapture.

THE OLD MAN

"The best of books, the one which preaches nothing
"but equality, friendship, humility and concord, the
"Gospel, has, for centuries, served as a pretext for the
"fury of Europeans. How many public and private
"tyrannies are still practised on earth in its name!
"Who then will boast that he is useful to his fellow men
"because of a book? Remember the fate of most
"of the philosophers who have preached them wisdom.
"Homer, who has clothed it in such splendid verses,
"lived by alms. Socrates, who gave the Athenians
"such friendly lessons in wisdom in his discourses
"and by his morality, was judicially poisoned by them.
"His sublime disciple, Plato, was condemned to slavery
"by order of the very prince who protected him;
"and, before their time, Pythagoras, who broadened
"the concept of humanity to include animals,
"was burnt alive by the inhabitants of Croton.
"Besides, most of these famous names themselves
"have come down to us deformed by some satirical
"traits which characterize them, man's ingratitude
"taking pleasure in identifying them in that way;

"and if, in that crowd, the fame of some of them has
"come down to us pure and unblemished, it is
"because those who have enjoyed it have lived far
"from the society of their contemporaries: very much
"like those statues which are dug out of the soil in
"Greece and in Italy and which escaped the fury of
"the barbarians because they had been buried in the
"entrails of the earth".

"From this you can see that, to acquire the tumult-
"uous fame of scholarship, one needs plenty of cour-
"age and must be prepared to sacrifice one's life.
"Besides, do you suppose that in France this fame
"inspires interest in the wealthy? They care little for
"the scholars whose learning brings neither honours to
"their native land, nor a place in the government, nor
"introduction to Court! In these days of general indiffe-
"rence to everything, save wealth and sensual pleasure,
"there is little persecution: knowledge and virtue lead
"to no distinction, because everything in the State is
"paid for. In former times, they earned sure rewards
"through appointment to various offices in the Church,
"the Magistracy or Government: today, they only
"serve for the writing of books. But this fruit of their
"labours, if of little value to a man of the world, is
"always worthy of its divine origin. It is these books
"which are destined, in particular, to give lustre to an
"obscure life, to comfort the unhappy, to enlighten
"nations, and to tell the truth to kings themselves. It is,
"beyond doubt, the most sacred function on earth with

"which Heaven may honour a mortal. Who is the man
"who does not find solace from the injustice and con-
"tempt of those who command wealth, at the thought
"that his work will live on, from century to century,
"and from one nation to another, to serve as a barrier
"against sin and against tyrants; and that, from the
"midst of the gloom where he spent his life, there
"will spring a glory which will throw into the shade
"that of most kings, whose monuments sink into
"oblivion, despite the flatterers who exalt and praise
"them ?".

PAUL

"Ah! I would desire that fame only to cast it on
"Virginie, and to endear her to the universe. But tell
"me, you who possess such wide learning, whether
"we shall be married some day. I should like to be
"learned, were it only to foresee the future.

THE OLD MAN

"Who would wish to live, son, if he knew the future?
"A single misfortune that we anticipate gives us so
"many vain anxieties! Knowledge of an impending
"disaster would ruin all the intervening days. We should
"not even examine too deeply what surrounds us;
"and Heaven, which gave us the faculty of reflection
"to anticipate our needs, has provided those needs
"to set limits to our reflection."

PAUL

"With money, so you say, one, in Europe, can "acquire titles and honours. I shall go and earn a "fortune in Bengal, and then proceed to Paris to "marry Virginie. I am going to sail".

THE OLD MAN

"What! do you mean to say that you would "abandon her mother and your own?"

PAUL

"You have yourself advised me to travel to India".

THE OLD MAN

"Virginie was here at the time. But you are now the "sole support of your mother and of hers".

PAUL

"Virginie will assist them through her wealthy "relative".

THE OLD MAN

"The rich rarely assist the poor, unless the latter

"pay homage to them in society. They have relatives
"of their own more worthy of pity than Madame de
"La Tour, who, for lack of assistance from them,
"sacrifice their freedom for the sake of a sustenance
"and spend their life cloistered in monasteries".

PAUL

"What a country is Europe! Oh! Virginie must
"return. What need has she of a wealthy relative!
"She was so happy in these huts, so beautiful and so
"gracefully trimmed with a red kerchief and with
"a crown of flowers! Oh! return, Virginie, leave
"your mansions and your grandeurs. Return to
"these rocks, in the shade of these woods and of
"our coconut trees. Alas! you are perhaps unhappy
"now!"— And he began to weep. "Father, do not
"conceal anything from me; if you are unable to
"tell me if I shall marry Virginie, tell me at least
"if she still loves me in spite of those noblemen
"who speak to the king and go and visit her"

THE OLD MAN

"Oh! my friend! I have no doubt that she loves
"you, for several reasons, but, first of all, because
"she is virtuous". On hearing these words, he threw
his arms round my neck in a transport of delight.

PAUL

"But do you believe that European women are as
"insincere as they are depicted in comedies and in
"the books you lent me?"

THE OLD MAN

"Women are deceitful in countries where men are
"tyrants. Violence breeds guile"

PAUL

"How can anybody be a tyrant to women?"

THE OLD MAN

"In makihg them marry without consulting their
"wishes: a young girl to an old man, a sensitive
"woman to an indifferent man".

PAUL

"Why not marry those who are well suited for
"each other: the young to the young, the passionate
"to their like?"

THE OLD MAN

"The difficulty is that, in France, most young men
"have not the means to marry, and that they only
"acquire wealth when they grow old. When they are

"young, they seduce their neighbours' wives, and,
"when they are old, they are unable to retain the
"affection of their spouses. Those who betrayed when
"they were young, are betrayed in their old age.
"This is one of the reactions of that universal justice
"which governs the world: one excess always counter-
"balances another. So, most Europeans spend their
"life in this state of double irregularity, and this
"increases in a society as riches accumulate in fewer
"hands. The State is like a garden where small trees
"cannot grow if there are tall ones about which keep
"them in their shade; but there exists this difference
"that the beauty of a garden may be created by a
"small number of large trees, while the welfare of a
"State always depends on the multitude and equality
"of its subjects, and not on a small number of wealthy
"subjects."

PAUL

"But why need one be rich to get married?"

THE OLD MAN

"In order to spend one's days in opulence, without
"working".

PAUL

"But why not work? Do I not work?"

THE OLD MAN

"The point is that, in Europe, manual work is
"considered degrading: it is called mechanical work.
"Working the land is deemed the most contemptible
"of all occupations. A craftsman there is held in much
"higher esteem than a peasant."

PAUL

"What! the art which feeds mankind is depised
"in Europe? I don't understand you".

THE OLD MAN

"Oh! it is impossible for a man brought up accord-
"ing to nature to understand the depravity of society.
"One forms a very precise idea of order, but not of
"disorder. Beauty, virtue, happiness have proportions;
"deformity, vice and misery have none".

PAUL

"The rich then are very happy; nothing constitutes
"an obstacle for them. They can shower favours on
"the objects of their delight."

THE OLD MAN

"Most of them have lost the sense of enjoyment

"by the fact that they obtain everything without the
"slightest effort. Have you not noticed that the delight
"we find in rest is acquired by fatigue; in eating, by
"hunger; and in drinking, by thirst? Well! that of
"loving and being loved is only acquired by countless
"privations and sacrifices. Riches deprive the wealthy
"of these pleasures by anticipating their wants. Add,
"to the boredom that follows on satiety, the
"arrogance born of opulence and which the sligh-
"test deprivation offends, even if the most intense
"joys have ceased to humour them. The pleasure
"derived from the fragrance of a thousand roses only
"lasts a moment; but the pain caused by a single
"one of their thorns long outlasts the sting. One
"evil in the midst of their pleasures, is, to the rich,
"like a thorn among roses. To the poor, on the
"contrary, a pleasure in the midst of evils is a flower
"among thorns: they savour every bit of joy. All
"effect is heightened by contrast. Nature has balanced
"all things. All told, what state would you think
"preferable: having next to no hope and everything
"to fear, or, alternatively, next to nothing to fear and
"everything to hope for? The former situation is that
"of the rich, the latter that of the poor. But these ex-
"tremes are equally difficult to bear for man, whose
"happiness consists in mediocrity and virtue".

PAUL

"What do you understand by virtue?"

THE OLD MAN

"Son, you who support your parents by your work,
"need no definition of virtue. Virtue is an effort made
"at our own expense for the good of others, with the
"view of being agreeable to God alone."

PAUL

"Oh! how virtuous is Virginie! It is out of virtue
"that she wanted to be rich, so as to be generous.
"It is out of virtue that she left this island: virtue
"will bring her back".

The thought of her approaching return fired
the imagination of the young man and all his anxieties
vanished. Virginie had not written because she
would be arriving shortly. It took such a short time
from Europe with a favourable wind! He enumerated
the vessels which had made the journey of four
thousand five hundred leagues in less than three
months. The vessel that she had sailed on would
need no more than two. Builders were so clever
nowadays and sailors so skilful! He spoke of his
arrangements for the reception he would give her, of
the new lodging he would build, of the joys and the
surprises he would provide for her each day when she
was his wife. His wife!— the very thought of it
entranced him. "At least, father", he told me, "you
"will do no work henceforth except for your pleasure.

"Virginie being rich, we shall have many slaves
"who will labour for you. You will always be with us,
"having no other care but to enjoy life and be
"happy". And, beyond himself, he went and communicated to his family the joy with which his heart was overflowing.

Within a short time, grave misgivings followed on high hopes. Violent passions always cast our soul from one extreme to the other. It often happened that, on the following day, Paul returned to me, overcome by sorrow. He would tell me: "Virginie does
"not write to me. If she had left Europe, she would
"have advised me of her departure. Ah! the rumours
"that have spread concerning her are only too well
"founded! Her aunt has married her to some noble-
"man. The love of riches has been her ruin as that
"of so many others".
"In those books which describe women so truly,
"virtue is only a theme for romance. Had Virginie been
"virtuous, she would not have left her own mother
"and myself. While I spend my life thinking of her,
"she forgets me. While I grieve, she is enjoying
"herself. Ah! this thought drives me to despair.
"All work annoys me, all company bores me. Would
"to God war was declared in India! I would go there
"to die".
"Son", I replied "the courage that drives us to court
"death is but the courage of a moment. It is often

"excited by the vain applause of men. There is another
"which is less common and more necessary and which
"enables us to support life's misfortunes day after
"day, with none to witness or to praise: and this
"is patience. It takes its support, not from the opinion
"of others, nor from the impulse of our passions,
"but from God's will. Patience is the courage of
"virtue".

"Ah!" he exclaimed "so I am not virtuous. Every-
"thing overwhelms and depresses me".

"Virtue", I rejoined, "uniform, constant and
"unalterable, is not the lot of man. In the midst of so
"many passions which disturb us, our reason becomes
"confused and obscured; but there are beacons at
"whose light we can revive its flame, and these are
"summed up in one word: literature."

"Literature, my son, is a deliverance sent to us
"from heaven. It is a ray of that wisdom which
"governs the universe, and which man, inspired
"by some divine art, has learnt to retain on earth.
"Like the rays of the sun, it illuminates, delights
"and inflames: it is a heavenly light. Like fire, it
"subdues everything to our use: thanks to it we
"gather around us things, places, men and time.
"It reminds us of the principles of human life. It
"soothes passions and represses vice. It stimulates
"virtues by the venerable examples of righteous men
"whom it extols, and whose images, always held in
"high honour, it places before us. It is a daughter

"of Heaven who comes down on earth to alleviate
"the misfortunes of mankind. The famous writers
"whom it inspires have invariably revealed themselves
"during the ages which were most difficult for any
"society to bear, ages of barbarity or of depravity.
"Son, books have comforted countless men more
"miserable than you are: Xenophon, exiled from
"his native land after leading back home ten thousand
"of his fellow Greeks; Scipio Africanus, weary of
"the calumnies of the Romans, and Lucullus, of their
"intrigues; Catinat, of the ingratitude of his monarch.
"The Greeks, who were so ingenious, had ascribed
"to each of the Muses who preside over literary
"achievements a section of our intelligence for her
"to govern: we must, therefore, submit to them our
"passions to regulate by imposing a yoke and a curb
"on them. With respect to the powers of our soul,
"they should discharge the same duties as the Hours
"who harnessed and drove the horses of the Sun.
"You should read, my son. The sages who wrote
"before our time are travellers who have preceded
"us along the paths of misfortune, who hold out
"a hand and invite us to join their company when
"everything forsakes us. A good book is a good
"friend".

"Ah!" exclaimed Paul "there was no need for me
"to know how to read when Virginie was here. She
"had studied no more than I had; but, when she

"looked at me, calling me her friend, it was impossible
"for me to experience any sorrow".

"No doubt", I said, "there can be no companion
"more agreeable than a loving mistress. There is,
"besides, in woman, a light cheerfulness which
"dispels the sadness of man. Her graces dissipate
"the dark ghosts of reflection. Her countenance
"attracts by its charms and inspires confidence.
"What joy is not enhanced by her joy? What brow
"does not relax when she smiles? What fury can
"resist her tears? Virginie will return with more
"philosophy than you have. She will be greatly
"surprised not to find the garden completely re-
"instated, she who always dreams of embellishing it,
"in spite of her relative's harassments, far from her
"mother and from you".

The thought of Virginie's approaching return renewed Paul's courage and brought him back to his rural occupations, happy, in the midst of his labours, to provide his work with a purpose which suited his passion.

One morning, at daybreak (this was on the 24th of December 1744) Paul, as he arose, noticed a white flag hoisted on the *Montagne de la Découverte*. This flag signalled a vessel that could be seen at sea. He ran to town to enquire if it was not bringing news of Virginie. He stayed there until the return of the harbour pilot who, as was customary, had gone on board to reconnoitre. This man only returned in the evening. He reported to the Governor that the vessel was the *St. Géran*, a seven hundred tonner, under the command of a captain, Mr. Aubin; that it was four leagues out at sea, and that it would only cast anchor in Port Louis harbour the following day, after dinner, if the wind was favourable. Not a breeze was blowing then. The pilot handed over to the Governor the letters which this vessel had brought from France. There was one for Madame de La Tour, in Virginie's handwriting. Paul, immediately, caught hold of it, kissed it with ectasy, placed it in his bosom and ran back to the plantation. From the farthest point from which he could see the family awaiting his return, on the *Rocher des Adieux*, he held the letter up in the air, unable to say a word; and everybody immediately gathered round Madame de La Tour to hear it read. Virginie informed her mother that she had suffered considerable hardship at the hands of her aunt, who had wanted to marry her against her inclination, had then disinherited her, and had finally sent her away, at a time when she could not reach the *Isle de France* otherwise than during the cyclone season; that she had attempted in vain to appease her by explaining what she owed to her mother and to habits contracted during her tender age; only to be called a senseless girl whose head was turned by the reading of novels; that she was now looking forward to nothing but the joy of seeing and embracing her dear family, and she would have gratified this earnest wish on that very day, had the captain allowed her to embark in the pilot's launch; but that he had objected to her leaving the ship because of the distance which separated it from land, and because of the rough sea which prevailed off the coast, in spite of the stillness of the wind.

The reading of the letter was scarcely completed when the whole family exclaimed, overcome with joy: "**Virginie** has arrived!" mistresses and servants all embraced one another. Madame de La Tour said to Paul: "Son, go and inform our neighbour of Virginie's "arrival". Domingue immediately lit a torch "and he and Paul made their way to my house.

It might have been ten in the evening. I had just put out my lamp and gone to bed, when across the palisade of my hut, I noticed a light in the woods. Forthwith, I heard Paul calling me. I rose and had no sooner dressed than Paul, beside himself and out of breath, jumped at my neck and embraced me, saying "Let us go! let us go! Virginie has arrived, let us go "down to the harbour; the vessel will anchor at "dawn".

We immediately set out on our way. As we were passing through the woods of *Montagne Longue*, well on our way from Pamplemousses to the harbour, I heard steps behind me. It was a negro who was advancing at long strides. As he reached us, I enquired whence he came and whither he was going in such haste. He replied: "I am coming from the district called *Poudre d'Or:* I have been sent to the harbour "to inform the Governor that a vessel coming from "France has cast anchor on the leeward side of "*Ile d'Ambre*. It is firing a distress gun because the "sea is extremely rough". Having said this, the man pursued his way without further delay.

I then said to Paul: "Let us proceed to the district "of *Poudre d'Or* to meet Virginie: it is only three "leagues from here". We hastened towards the north of the island. The heat was sweltering. The moon had risen, and around it three large black circles appeared. The sky was dismally dark. We could discern, with the frequent glimmer of lightning, long rows of thick clouds, gloomy and low, accumulating about the centre of the island, blown from the sea, at great speed, although the least wind could not be felt on land. On our way, we thought we heard claps of thunder, but, after listening intently, we realized that it was the report of a gun repeated by the echoes. These distant sounds adding their effect to the threatening aspect of thunder clouds made me shudder. I had no doubt that they were alarm signals from a ship in distress. Half an hour later, we ceased hearing these shots altogether; and this silence appeared to me more terrifying than the dismal noise which had preceded it.

We hastened forward without a word, and without daring communicate to each other our apprehensions. About midnight, streaming with perspiration we reached the seashore in the district of *Poudre d'Or*. The waves were crashing with a dreadful noise, covering the rocks and the shoals with foam of a dazzling whiteness and with sparks of fire. In spite of the darkness, we could, in this phosphoric glimmer, distinguish the fishermen's pirogues which had been pulled high up on the sand beach.

At some distance on the border of the wood, we saw a fire around which several settlers had gathered We went there to rest, waiting for the break of day. While we were seated near this fire, one of these settlers related that in the afternoon he had seen a vessel on the high sea being driven on to the coast by the currents; night had concealed it from his sight; two hours after sunset, he had heard it firing shots, calling for help; but that the sea was so stormy that it had been impossible to launch a boat to approach it. After a while, he thought he had seen its lanterns and, in that case, he feared that the vessel, driven so near to the shore, had passed between the mainland and the small *Ile d'Ambre*, mistaking the latter for the *Coin de Mire* near which vessels pass before entering Port Louis. If such was the case, he added, a fact which he could not affirm, this vessel was exposed to the greatest peril. Another settler spoke next and told us that he had on several occasions crossed the channel which separates *Ile d'Ambre* from the coast, that he had made soundings and that its anchorage was quite good, and that the vessel was as safe there as in the best of harbours.

"I could load all my fortune in it", he added, "and sleep on board as soundly as on land". A third man said that it would have been impossible for the vessel to enter the channel where even small crafts had difficulty in sailing. He gave the assurance that he had seen it anchor beyond *Ile d'Ambre* : so that, if the wind arose in the morning, it would be free either to put out to sea or to enter the harbour. Others expressed different opinions. While they were debating with one another, after the custom of idle creoles, Paul and I observed the most complete silence. We stayed until early dawn : but there was not enough light in the sky to enable us to perceive any object in the sea which, besides, was wrapped in a shroud of mist. Out at sea, we saw nothing but what seemed a dark cloud; but this we were told, was *Ile d'Ambre*, lying off the coast about a quarter of a league away. In this gloom, we could only see the extremity of the shore where we were standing, and some mountain peaks inland, which were visible at intervals among the clouds which moved around them.

About seven in the morning, we heard in the woods the beating of drums : it was the Governor, M. de La Bourdonnaye, who was arriving on horseback, followed by a detachment of soldiers armed with rifles, and by a large number of planters and negroes.

He stationed his soldiers on the shore and ordered them to fire simultaneously. They had no sooner discharged their rifles than we noticed a light at sea, followed almost immediately by the sound of a gun. We estimated that the vessel was a short distance from us, and we all ran towards the spot where we had seen the signal. We then discerned, through the mist, the hull and the yards of a large vessel. We were so close to it that, in spite of the noise of the waves, we could hear the whistle of the boatswain who commanded the manœuvre and the cries of the sailors who shouted three times : Long live the King ! for this is the cry of all Frenchmen, when in extreme danger and in intense joy : as if in the hour of peril, they called their sovereign to their rescue, or declared their readiness to give their life for him.

From the moment when the *St. Géran* found that we were near enough to bring aid, it did not cease to fire, at intervals of three minutes. M. de La Bourdonnaye ordered the lighting of fires, at different points on the beach, and sent men to fetch provisions, planks, hawsers and empty casks from all the inhabitants in the neighbourhood. A crowd of settlers soon arrived, accompanied by their servants, loaded with provisions and rigging sent by the inhabitants of *Poudre d'Or*, *Flacq* and *Rivière du Rempart*. One of the oldest inhabitants approached the Governor and said to him : "Sir, all night, we have heard "rumbling noises in the mountain; in the woods, the

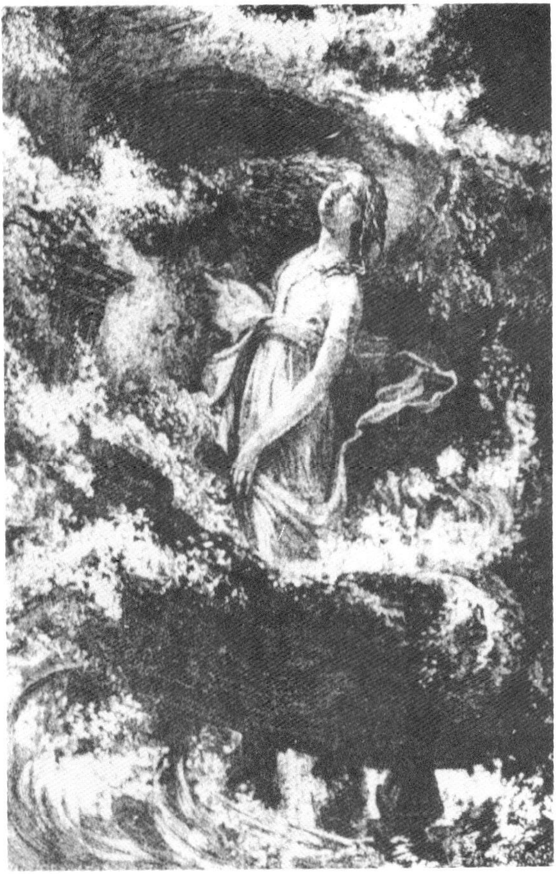

"leaves on the trees are astir, although there is no "wind; sea birds seek refuge on land; all these signs "certainly portend a hurricane". "Well my friends" the Governor replied, "we are ready for it and so "is the vessel, no doubt".

In fact, everything foreshadowed the approach of a hurricane. The clouds which we saw at the zenith were dismally dark in the centre and copper-coloured round their edges. The air was ringing with the cries of phaetons, frigate birds, shearwaters and numbers of sea birds, which, in spite of the prevailing darkness, were coming from all points on the horizon to seek shelter on the island.

About nine in the morning, frightening noises were heard in the direction of the sea, as if torrents of water mingled with claps of thunder were rolling down from the mountain top. Everybody exclaimed : "The hurricane is on us !" and, that very moment, a fearful whirlwind carried away the mist which covered *Ile d'Ambre* and its channel. The *St. Géran* then appeared, crowded with people, her yards and topmasts lowered on deck, her flag at half-mast, four hawsers afore and one aft to hold her stern. She had anchored between *Ile d'Ambre* and the mainland, within the circle of reefs which surrounds the Isle de France, and which she had cleared at a spot where no vessel had ever passed before. Her prow was fronting the waves rushing from the high seas, and each of those which penetrated the channel, raised her whole stern above the water, so that her keel was in the air; but, with this motion, the stern, happening to plunge, disappeared from view up to the taffrail, as if it was submerged. In that situation, the wind and the sea driving her towards the land, made it equally impossible for the vessel to move back the way she had come, or, severing her hawsers, to run aground on the beach from which she was separated by shallow waters studded with reefs.

Each wave, crashing against the coast, advanced with a roar to the extremity of the bays, and projected stones more than fifty feet inland; then, as it receded, it uncovered a large part of the foundation of the shore, where it rattled the pebbles with a hoarse and frightening noise. The sea, stirred by the wind, was constantly swelling, and the whole channel comprised between this island and *Ile d'Ambre* was but a vast sheet of white foam, furrowed with deep waves. That foam gathered at the inner ends of the bays, reaching a height of over six feet, and the wind, which swept its surface, carried it beyond the steep slope of the shore, more than half a league inland. These innumerable white flakes, blown horizontally as far as the foot of the mountains, looked like snow issuing from the sea. The horizon presented every sign of a great hurricane and the sea was indistinguishable from the sky. Hideously shaped clouds were continually breaking away from it, running across the zenith with the speed of birds, while others seemed stationary, like huge rocks. No azure portion of the sky was revealed; only a wan and olive coloured glimmer threw some light over every object on earth, in the sea and in the sky.

With the rocking of the vessel, what we dreaded happened : the fore cables snapped, and, held in position by one hawser only, the vessel was thrown on the rocks at half a cable's length from the shore. A cry of anguish arose from us all. Paul was about to rush into the sea, when I held him by the arm. "Son", I said "do you wish to perish" ? "Let me "go and rescue her, or let me die !" he exclaimed. Despair deprived him of judgment, and, to save him from rushing to his doom, Domingue and I tied a long rope round his waist, holding one end of it. Paul then proceeded towards the *St. Géran*, now swimming and now treading on the reefs. Sometimes, he could hope that he would reach his goal, because the sea, with its irregular movements, left the vessel almost high and dry, so that one could have gone round her on foot; but the next moment, rushing again with increased fury, huge waves covered her with masses of water which lifted the front of her keel and threw back high on the beach the unfortunate Paul, his legs bleeding, his chest all bruised and half drowned.

No sooner had he recovered his senses than he

got up and rushed back with renewed vigour towards the vessel which the sea was tearing apart with horrible shocks. The whole crew, then despairing of their safety, were jumping into the sea, on yards, planks, chicken coops, tables and casks. We then witnessed a scene worthy of eternal pity : a young lady appeared on the stern-gallery of the *St. Géran*, holding out her arms towards him who was striving so hard to reach her. It was Virginie. By his intrepidity, she had recognized her lover. The sight of this charming girl exposed to such terrible danger filled us with sorrow and despair. With a dignified and courageous gesture, Virginie was waving her hand, as if to bid us an eternal farewell. All the sailors had jumped into the sea. The only one left on deck was all naked, with muscles like those of Hercules. He approached Virginie with respect : we saw him falling to her knees and endeavouring to rid her of her clothes, but, pushing him aside with dignity she, turned her eyes away from him. We then heard the spectators shouting repeatedly : "Oh ! save her, "save her, do not leave her". That very moment, a frightening mass of water rushed between *Ile d'Ambre* and the coast and advanced with a roar towards the vessel which it threatened with its dark flanks and foaming crests.

At this terrifying sight, the sailor gave up and jumped overboard and Virginie, seeing that death was inevitable, rested a hand on her clothes, the other on her heart, and raising her eyes in serene ecstasy, she seemed an angel poised to take her flight to heaven.

Oh! hateful day! Alas! everything was swallowed up. The waves threw back far inland some of the spectators whom a humanitarian impulse had persuaded to advance towards Virginie, as well as the sailor who had wished to save her by swimming to shore with her. This man, who had escaped certain death, fell on his knees on the shore saying: "Oh! "God! you have saved my life! but I would have "gladly given it for the noble lady who never consented "to take her clothes off in my sight". Domingue and I pulled the unfortunate Paul, senseless, out of the water, bleeding from his mouth and ears. The Governor ordered that he should be entrusted to the care of the surgeons, and we, on our side, made searches along the beach, to find out if the sea did not bring back Virginie's corpse; but the wind having turned suddenly, as frequently happens in hurricanes, we thought with sorrow that we would not even be able to perform funeral rites for the unfortunate girl. We left this spot, overwhelmed by consternation, all of us affected by the loss of a single person, in a shipwreck in which many perished, and most of us after witnessing such a cruel end befalling such a virtuous girl, doubting the existence of a Providence; for some calamities are so tragic and so little deserved, that hope is shaken even in the heart of the wise.

In the meantime, Paul, who was beginning to recover his senses, had been placed in a neighbouring house, until he was fit to be transferred to his own. For my part, I returned with Domingue, to prepare Virginie's mother and her friend for the news of this disaster. When we had reached the entrance to the vale of *Rivière des Lataniers*, some negroes told us that the sea was rejecting plenty of wreckage from the ship in the bay opposite. We went there, and one of the first things I saw on the beach was Virginie's corpse. She was half covered with sand, in the very attitude in which we had seen her perish. Her features were not considerably altered. Her eyes were closed, but serenity was still on her brow: only, the pale violets of death were blended on her cheeks with the rose of bashfulness. One of her hands was resting on her clothes, and the other, which she was pressing against her heart, was firmly closed and rigid. With difficulty I succeeded in extricating from it a small box; but how great was my surprise when I discovered that it contained the portrait of Paul, which she had promised never to part with as long as she lived. At this last proof of the faithfulness and love of this unfortunate girl, I shed bitter tears. As for Domingue, he was beating his breast and piercing the air with his doleful cries. We carried the body of Virginie to a fisherman's hut, where we entrusted it to the care of some Indian women who undertook to dress it. While they were performing this mournful service, we walked up to the plantation. There we found Madame de La Tour and Marguerite praying, while awaiting for news of the vessel. As soon as Madame de La Tour saw me, she exclaimed : "Where is my daughter, "my darling daughter, my child ?" My silence and my tears leaving no room for doubt, she was suddenly seized by fits of suffocation and painful anguish, while from her voice, only sighs and sobs escaped. As for Marguerite, she exclaimed : "Where is my "son ? I do not see my son !" and fainted.

We ran to her; and, having revived her, I gave her the assurance that Paul was alive and that the Governor had caused him to be attended to. She recovered only to assist her friend who had long and frequent fainting fits. Madame de La Tour spent the whole night in a state of cruel suffering; and, by the length of these fits, I understood that no grief can be as intense as that of a mother. When she regained consciousness, she turned her mournful gaze steadily to heaven. In vain her friend and ourselves pressed her hands in ours, in vain we called her by the most loving names; she seemed insensitive to these manifestations of our old affection and nothing but muffled groans came from her oppressed bosom.

Early in the morning, Paul was brought in, lying on a palankeen. He had recovered the use of his senses; but he was unable to utter a word. His meeting with his mother and Madame de La Tour, which I had dreaded at first, achieved more than all the solicitude I had hitherto shown. A glimmer of consolation appeared on the brow of these two unfortunate mothers. They both stood by his side, clasping him in their arms and kissing him, and their tears, which had hitherto been restrained by the violence of their grief, began to flow. Paul soon added his tears to theirs. Nature having thus found deliverance in these three unfortunate creatures, a long drowsiness succeeded the convulsions of grief and lulled them into a death-like lethargy.

M. de La Bourdonnaye had me informed in secret that the body of Virginie had been taken to town on his orders, and would thence be transferred to the church of Pamplemousses. I immediately went down to Port Louis where I found a crowd coming from all the districts to attend her funeral, as if this island had lost in Virginie her most precious possession. The ships in harbour had placed their yards athwart, flying their flags at half-mast and firing guns at long intervals. Grenadiers led the convoy. They had sloped their rifles, the drums veiled with mourning crape, uttered none but mournful sounds and consternation was painted in the features of these very warriors who so often had braved death on the battlefield with unchanged countenance. Eight young maidens from the most influential families, dressed in white and holding palms in their hands, carried the body of their virtuous companion overspread with flowers. A choir of young children followed, singing hymns; next came all the most distinguished inhabitants of the island and members of its general staff, after whom the Governor came on foot, followed by the common people in their multitude.

This is what the Governor had decreed, to pay homage to the virtues of Virginie. But when her body had reached the foot of this mountain, within view of these same huts where she had for so long spread happiness, and which her loss was now filling with despair, the whole funeral pageant broke up: hymns and chants ceased; nothing but sighing and sobbing could be heard throughout the plain. Groups of young maidens were seen rushing from the neighbouring plantations bringing handkerchiefs, strings of beads and flower wreaths with which to touch the coffin of Virginie while invoking her as a Saint. Mothers were praying to God for such a daughter; boys, for as faithful a sweetheart, the poor for as generous a friend, and slaves for as kind a mistress.

When she had reached the place of burial, negresses from Madagascar, and Kafirs from Mozambique, according to their native custom deposited baskets of fruit around her and hung pieces of cloth to the neighbouring trees, Indian women from Bengal and from the coast of Malabar, brought cages full of birds which they liberated over her body: so true it is that the loss of a lovable creature is a concern for all nations! and such is the power of unfortunate virtue which unites all religions about its grave!

Guards had to be placed near the open grave to keep away some girls from poor families, who would have thrown themselves in it at all costs saying that they no longer had any consolation to expect in this world, and that there was nothing left for them but to die with their sole benefactress.

She was interred near the Church of Pamplemousses, on its western side, close to a bamboo grove where she loved to rest at the side of the one whom she called her brother, whenever she came with her mother and Marguerite to attend mass.

Returning from the funeral ceremony, M. de La Bourdonnaye came here, followed by part of his retinue. He offered Madame de La Tour and her friend all the assistance that it was in his power to give. He expressed himself in few words, but with indignation, against the cruel aunt, and, approaching Paul, he used words which he thought likely to comfort him: "I wished" he said "your happiness "and that of your family. I take God to witness. "My friend, you must go to France, I shall see to it "that you are given a commission. In your absence "I shall take care of your mother as if she were mine". Saying so, he held out his hand, but Paul drew back his own and turned aside to avoid seeing him.

As for me, I stayed in the house of my ill-fated

friends to give them, as well as Paul, every assistance I was capable of. After three weeks, Paul was strong enough to walk, but his sorrow seemed to increase in proportion to his returning strength. He was indifferent to everything; his eyes were dull, and he failed to answer questions. Madame de La Tour, who was dying, often told him : "My son, as "long as I see you, I shall imagine that I am seeing "my dear Virginie". At the name of Virginie, he would shudder and move away from her, in spite of the requests of his mother who called him back to her friend. He would retire to the garden and sit at the foot of Virginie's coconut tree, his eyes fixed on her fountain. The Governor's surgeon who had taken the greatest care of him and of the ladies, told us that to rescue him from his depressed mood, we should leave him free to do what he pleased without interference, as this was the only means of overcoming the silence he persisted in.

I resolved to follow his advice. As soon as Paul felt his strength coming back the first use he made of it was to leave the plantation. As I did not wish to lose sight of him, I set out after him, requesting Domingue to take some provisions and accompany us. As the young man came down from the hill, his spirits and strength gradually seemed to revive. He first took the road to Pamplemousses and, when he was near the church, in the avenues bordered by bamboos, he made straight for the spot when he saw that the earth had recently been disturbed; and there, on his knees, his eyes raised to heaven, he prayed for a long time. His behaviour seemed to me to augur well for the return of his senses, since this mark of confidence in the Supreme Being showed that his mind was beginning to recover its normal faculties. Domingue and I also knelt down, following his example, and joined in prayer. Then he rose, and directed his steps towards the north of the island, without paying much attention to us. As I knew that he was ignorant of the place where the body of Virginie had been laid or even whether it had been rescued from the sea, I asked him why he had gone to pray at the foot of those bamboos, and he answered : "We had so often been there together".

He proceeded as far as the verge of the forest, where night overtook us. There, I persuaded him to follow my example and take some nourishment; we then slept on the grass under a tree. The following day, I thought he would decide to trace his steps back. In fact, he looked for some time towards the plain where stood the church of Pamplemousses, with its long avenues of bamboos and began moving as if to return there : but then, suddenly, plunged into the forest, walking steadily towards the north. I guessed what he had in mind and I endeavoured in vain to dissuade him. We reached the district of *Poudre d'Or* at about noon. He went down hurriedly to the seashore, opposite the place where the *St.*

Geran had sunk. At the sight of *Ile d'Ambre* and of the channel, which was then as smooth as a mirror, he exclaimed: "Oh ! Virginie, my dearest Virginie !" and, immediately, fell down unconscious. Domingue and I carried him inside the forest where, with considerable difficulty , we revived him. As soon as he had recovered consciousness, he insisted on returning to the shore, but I entreated him not to renew his sorrow and ours by such cruel reminiscences, and he went along another course. During the next eight days, he visited all the places where he had been with the companion of his childhood. We went along the path by which she had gone to beg for pardon on behalf of the slave from *Riviere Noire* : he again saw the banks of *Trois Mamelles* River, where she had rested when she could no longer walk, and that part of the wood where she had lost her way. All the spots which called back to his memory the anxieties, the games, the meals, and the kindness of his beloved, *Montagne Longue* River, my own little house, the neighbouring waterfall, the papaw tree she had planted, the lawns, where she loved to play, the clearings in the forest, where she loved to sing, all, in turn, brought tears into his eyes; and the very echoes which had, so often, been ringing with their mutual cries of joy, only repeated now those mournful words : "Virginie ! my dearest Virginie ".

As a result of the unsociable and roaming life he was leading, his eyes sank deep, his complexion

turned sallow, his health declined. Convinced that
the consciousness of our misfortunes increases with
the reminiscence of our pleasures, and that passions
grow more intense in solitude, I decided to remove
my unfortunate friend from the surroundings which
kept reminding him of his loss, and to transfer him to
some corner of the island where diversions were
plentiful. For his purpose, I took him to the inhabited
heights of the District of Plaines Wilhems, where he
had never been. Agriculture and commerce were
creating in that part of the island plenty of activity
and diversity. Gangs of carpenters were squaring
timber which others sawed into planks; carts were
coming and going along its roads, herds of cattle
and horses were grazing on its vast pasture grounds,
and the countryside was studded with houses. The
elevation of the ground allowed various sorts of
European plants to be grown in several places. Crops
of wheat could be seen here and there upon the plains,
carpets of strawberries in the clearings, and hedges
of roses along the roads. The freshness of the air,
while bracing the nerves, was even beneficial to the
health of Europeans. From these heights, almost
in the centre of the island, surrounded by vasts
forests, one could discern neither the sea, nor
Port Louis, nor the Church of Pamplemousses, nor
anything which could bring back to Paul recollections
of Virginie. Even the mountains which project several
spurs on the side overlooking Port Louis, present, on

the Plaines Wilhems side, but one vast promontory in a straight perpendicular line, from which arise tall pyramids of rock, round which clouds gather.

It was to these plains that I led Paul. I kept him on the move walking along with him in sunshine and rain alike, day and night, leading him purposely astray in the woods, in the cleared lands, in the fields, so as to divert his mind through the weariness of his body, and to distract his thoughts through his ignorance of the place and of the path from which we had strayed. But a lover's mind finds everywhere some trace of his beloved. Night and day, the silence of solitudes or the clamour of the plantations, time itself, which takes away in its course so many memories, nothing can take his mind away from her. Like a needle induced by contact with a magnet, it is shaken in vain and, when put at rest, turns to the pole which attracts it. Whenever I asked Paul, lost in the plains of Wilhems : "Where shall we go now ?" he would turn North and say: "There lie our mountains, let "us return to them".

I soon realised that all the means which I devised to deflect his attention were of no avail, and that I was left with no choice but to assail his passion itself by making use of all the resources of my feeble intellect. I, therefore, replied : "Yes, these are the "mountains where your dear Virginie dwelt, and this "is the portrait that you had given her, and which, "when dying, she was wearing close to her heart

"whose last throbbings were for you". I then showed
Paul the small portrait which he had offered Virginie
near the *Fontaine des Cocotiers*. When he saw it,
a distressing joy shone in his eyes. He eagerly seized
it with his feeble hands, and took it to his lips. Then
he suffocated with emotion, and in his bloodshot
eyes, tears were suspended, unable to flow.

"Son", I said, "listen to me, for I am your friend,
"and I have been Virginie's, and in the midst of
"your hopes, I have often tried to fortify your mind
"against the unforeseen accidents of life. What is it
"that you mourn with such bitterness ? Is it your
"own misfortune? Is it Virginie's? Your misfortune?
"yes, no doubt, it is considerable. You have lost the
"most lovable of girls, who would have proved the
"most worthy of wives. She had sacrificed her own
"interests to yours, and despising wealth, she had
"chosen you as being the only reward worthy of
"her virtue. But how do you know if she, from whom
"you were expecting such perfect happiness, would
"not have been for you the source of endless sorrow?
"She had no property, and she had been disowned:
"you had nothing to share with her but the proceeds
"of your labours. She had returned more delicate,
"by reason of her education, and more courageous,
"because of her misfortune, and you would have seen
"her wasting away day after day, striving to share your
"fatigues. Had she borne children to you, her anxieties
"and yours would have increased, from the difficulty

"of sustaining, alone with you, your elderly parents "and a growing family. You will say : "The Governor "would have assisted us." How can you tell whether "in a colony whose administrators change so fre- "quently, you will have other Labourdonnayes ? "Whether the commanders who come over will not "be men having neither morality nor ethics ? Whether "your wife, to obtain some paltry assistance, would "not have had to court their favours. Either she "would have been accessible and you would have "been worthy of pity; or else she would have been "virtuous and you would then have remained poor; "and lucky if, on account of her beauty and her "virtue, you had not been persecuted precisely by "those from whom you expected protection !"

"Still", you might say, "there would have remained "for me the satisfaction, independant of fortune, of "protecting the loved one whose attachment increases "in proportion to her weakness itself; of comforting "her with my own anxieties; of cheering her with my "sorrow, of fortifying our love with our mutual "suffering. No doubt, virtue and love enjoy these "bitter pleasures. But, she is no more; and you "still have those whom she loved best, next to you : "her mother and your own, whom your disconsolate "grief will lead to the grave. Make it your happiness "to assist them, as she had done herself. Son, charity "is the happiness of virtue; no other on earth is more "certain nor more intense. Dreams of pleasure, peace,

"joy, affluence, grandeur, are not made for that
"weak, itinerant, and shortlived creature : man.
"Consider how a step towards riches has hurled us all
"from one abyss to another. You opposed it, this is
"true; but who would have doubted that Virginie's
"voyage should have ended in her happiness and
"yours ? The invitation from a rich old relative, the
"advice of a wise Governor, the approval of a whole
"colony, the encouragement and authority of a
"priest, have brought about Virginie's ruin. And
"so we run forward to our loss, deceived by the very
"prudence of those who govern us. It would have been
"preferable, no doubt, not to trust them, nor to
"believe in the promptings and hopes of a deceitful
"world. But, after all, of so many men that we find
"busy in these plains, of so many others who go to
"India in quest of wealth, or of those who, without
"leaving their home, enjoy in Europe, the fruit of
"the work accomplished by the former, there is not a
"single one but is destined to lose, some day, what
"he cherishes above all, his rank, wealth, wife, children
"friends. Most of them will have to add to their loss
"the memory of their own imprudence. As for you,
"when you look within yourself, you find nothing to
"reproach yourself for: you have been true to your
"love. You have shown, in your early youth, the
"prudence of an experienced man in refusing to
"deviate from the love of nature. Your visions were
"the only correct ones, because they were pure,

"simple, disinterested, and because you had acquired
"sacred rights to Virginie that no fortune could
"outweigh. You have lost her, but not through im-
"prudence or covetousness, nor through your false
"judgment. It is God himself who made use of the
"passions of others to deprive you of the object of
"your love; God, from whom you hold all things,
"who knows your needs, and whose wisdom leaves
"no occasion for repentance and despair which only
"follow on evils that we ourselves have brought
"about".

"Here is what you can say to yourself in your mis-
"fortune : I have not deserved it. Is it then Virginie's
"fate, her death , her present state, that you deplore ?
"She has suffered the fate reserved to birth, beauty
"and nations themselves. The life of man, with all his
"designs, rises like a small tower, whose crowning
"is death. When she was born, she was doomed to die.
"She was happy in that she has untied the bonds
"of life before her mother and yours, before you; in
"other words, in that she did not die several deaths
"before the last !"

"Death, son, is a blessing for all men : it is the night
"of that restless day which we call life. It is in the
"sleep of death that all disease finds its everlasting rest,
"as do grief, sorrow, fears, which incessantly stir
"the wretched living. Consider the men who seem the
"happiest : you will see that they paid very dearly
"for this so-called happiness : public esteem, at the

"expense of domestic ills; wealth, with the loss of
"health; such a rare pleasure as that of being loved,
"by continual sacrifices : and, at the end of a life
"sacrificed to the interests of others, they often find
"themselves surrounded by none but false friends
"and ungrateful relations. But Virginie has been
"happy to the last. She was happy here with us,
"thanks to the blessings of nature; and, away from
"us, thanks to those of virtue; and even in that dread-
"ful instant when we saw her perish, she was still
"happy. For whether she cast her looks on a whole
"colony, which was in consternation on her account,
"or on you, who were striving with such dauntlessness
"to come to her aid, she must have seen how precious
"she was to all of us. She built up strength against
"the future by remembering the innocence of her life,
"and she received the prize which God sets apart for
"virtue, the gift of courage superior to danger. She
"faced death with serenity.

"Son, God has ascribed to virtue all the vicissitudes
"of life to bear, so as to show that she alone can
"withstand them, and in so doing, acquire happiness
"and fame. When He has high renown in store for
"her, He raises her on a lofty scene and exposes her
"to death; then her courage serves as an example,
"and the memory of her sufferings receives an undying
"tribute of tears from posterity. This is the imperisha-
"ble memorial reserved for her on this earth where all
"things must die and where the very memory of

"Kings is soon buried in eternal oblivion". But
"Virginie lives on. You see, son, everything on earth
"is subject to change, but nothing is lost. No human
"art could destroy the smallest particle of matter;
"could then something which was gifted with reason,
"sentiment, love, virtue, piety, perish, when the
"elements which clothe it are indestructible ? Ah !
"if Virginie was happy with us, she is far happier now.
"God exists, my son, and to this, the whole of Nature
"is witness : I need not prove it. Only the malice
"of man urges him to deny a jurisdiction which he
"dreads. Consciousness of His existence rests in
"your heart, just as His works are in front of your
"eyes. Can you believe then that He would leave
"Virginie unrewarded ? Do you believe that this
"same power which had enclosed such a noble heart
"within such a handsome frame, in which you could
"feel a divine work of art, could not have saved her
"from the waves ? That He who has organised man's
"present happiness according to laws unknown to
"you, could not organize a different one for Virginie
"according to laws which are equally unknown ?
"When we were in nothingness, had we been gifted
"with thought, could we have formed an idea of
"our existence ? And now that we live this obscure
"and fugitive life, can we foresee what lies beyond
"death, through which we are doomed to leave it ?
"Does God need, as man does, the small sphere
"which is our world, as a stage for His intelligence

"and His kindness; and is it only in the fields of
"Death that He can propagate human life ? There
"is not a single drop of water in the ocean but is full
"of living creatures which are dependant on us, and
"yet there would exist nothing for us among all
"those stars which revolve above our heads ! What !
"supreme intelligence and divine munificence would
"exist nowhere save where we are? and in all those
"radiant and innumerable spheres, in all those infinite
"spaces of light which surround them, and which
"neither storms nor nights can ever cloud, there
"would be nothing but empty space and eternal void?
"If we, who have created nothing by ourselves, dared
"assign limits to the power from whom we have
"received everything, we could believe that we are
"here on the boundaries of His dominions — where
"life is in conflict with death and, innocence with
"tyranny.

"No doubt, there does exist somewhere, a place
"where vitue receives its reward. Virginie is now at
"peace. Ah! if from the abode of angels she could be
"in correspondence with you, she would tell you, as
"she did in her farewell : Oh ! Paul, life is but an
"ordeal. I have been judged faithful to the laws of
"nature, of love and of virtue. I went beyond the seas
"in obedience to my parents, I gave up riches to remain
"faithful to my love and I chose to lose my life rather
"than outrage decency".

"**Heaven** had judged my life sufficiently full. I

"have for ever been spared poverty, calumny, storms
"and the sight of the suffering of others. None of the
"misfortunes that man dreads can touch me now;
"and you pity me! I am as pure and unchangeable as
"a particle of light; and you keep calling me back to
"the gloom of life ! Oh ! Paul, Oh ! my friend, re-
"member those happy days when we enjoyed the
"luxury of the morning sun shedding light on the
"peaks of these rocks, and spreading its rays over
"the heart of our forests. We felt raptures that we
"could not account for. In our simple wishes, we had
"wished to be all eyes, to enjoy the rich colours of
"dawn; all smell to scent the fragrance of our plants;
"all ears to hear the harmony of our birds; all heart,
"to be grateful for these benefits. Now, at the source
"of beauty, from which flows all that is enjoyable
"on earth, my soul sees, tastes, hears, touches, at
"once, what it could not have felt then, except
"through feeble senses. Ah ! what language could
"describe these shores of eternal brilliance which I
"inhabit for ever ? All that infinite power and Hea-
"venly generosity may have created to comfort an
"unfortunate being; all that harmony in a common
"ecstasy which proceeds from the friendship of in-
"numerable beings delighting in the same felicity, all
"these we enjoy in its purest form. You should, there-
"fore, bear the burden that has been assigned to you
"to intensify the felicity of your Virginie, with love
"that time will not destroy, by a union whose lights

"can never die. There, I shall allay your regrets, there,
"I shall wipe away your tears. Oh ! my friend, my
"young spouse ! lift up your soul to God in order to
"endure the evils of a moment".

My own emotion brought my speech to an end.
As for Paul, looking at me intently, he exclaimed :
"She is no more ! She is no more", and a long period
of langour followed on those melancholy words.
Then, on recovering, he said : "Since death is a
"blessing and Virginie is happy, I want to die too,
"and thus be united to her". And so, the grounds
of consolation I had invoked only served to nourish
his despair. I was like a man trying to save his friend
sinking to the bottom in the middle of a river and
refusing to swim.

Grief had overwhelmed him. Alas! The misfortunes
of our tender age prepare us for the hardships of
life, and Paul had never known any.

I brought him back to his cottage. There, I found
his mother and Madame de La Tour in a state of
depression which had intensified. Marguerite was
the more dejected. Lively temperaments which light
sorrows do not touch are those which offer the least
resistance to severe affliction.

"Oh ! my kind neighbour !" Marguerite, said to
me "I dreamt last night that I saw Virginie, dressed
"in white, among delightful groves and gardens.
"She said to me: "I enjoy a felicity worthy of envy".
"She then approached Paul with a smile on her lips,

"and she took him away with her. While striving to
"retain my son, I felt that I myself was quitting this
"earth, and that I followed him with unspeakable
"delight. I then desired to bid farewell to my friend,
"and I immediately saw her following us, with Marie
"and Domingue. But what I find still more surprising
"is that Madame de La Tour, that same night, had a
"dream characterized by identical circumstances."

"My friend", I replied, "I believe that nothing
happens in the world without God's permission.
"Dreams sometimes foreshadow the truth". Madame
de La Tour recounted an almost identical dream that
she had had that same night. I had never noticed any
propensity to superstition in any of these ladies; I
was therefore struck by the concordance of their
dreams and I had no doubt myself that these would
come true. This conviction that truth sometimes
occurs to us in our sleep, is widespread among all
peoples of the globe. The giants of history gave credit
to it; amongst others, Alexander, Caesar, the Scipios,
the Catos and Brutus, who were not men of weak
character. The Old Testament and the New provide
numerous instances of dreams which have come true
Personally, I need only draw on my own experience
in this respect; and I have felt more than once that
dreams are warnings from some spirit who takes an
interest in us. That if we try to deny or support,
with arguments, happenings which surpass human
understanding, **we are attempting the impossible.**

However, if man's intellect is only an image of that of God, since man has it in his power to promote his designs to the other end of the world by secret and disguised means, why should not the Supreme Being, who governs the universe, employ similar ways to achieve the same purpose ? A friend comforts his friend by means of a letter which travels through a number of countries, passes through national hatred, and brings joy and hope to one man; why could not the sovereign Protector of innocence come, by some secret way, to rescue a virtuous soul which places its trust in Him alone ? Does he need some outward sign to carry out His purpose, He who, in all His deeds, invariably operates by means of inward inspiration ? Why should we hesitate to believe in dreams ? Is life itself, full of so many vain and fugitive schemes, anything but a dream ?

However that may be, the dream of my unfortunate friends soon came true. Paul died two months after his dear Virginie, whose name was always on his lips. Marguerite saw her last hour approach, eight days after her son, with a joy such as none but virtue can feel. She bade the most loving farewell to Madame de La Tour, "with the hope" she said "of a peaceful "and everlasting reunion. Death is the greatest of "blessings", she added : "we should desire it. If life "is a chastisement, we should wish its end; if it is an "ordeal, we should pray that it be short".

The Government took charge of Domingue and

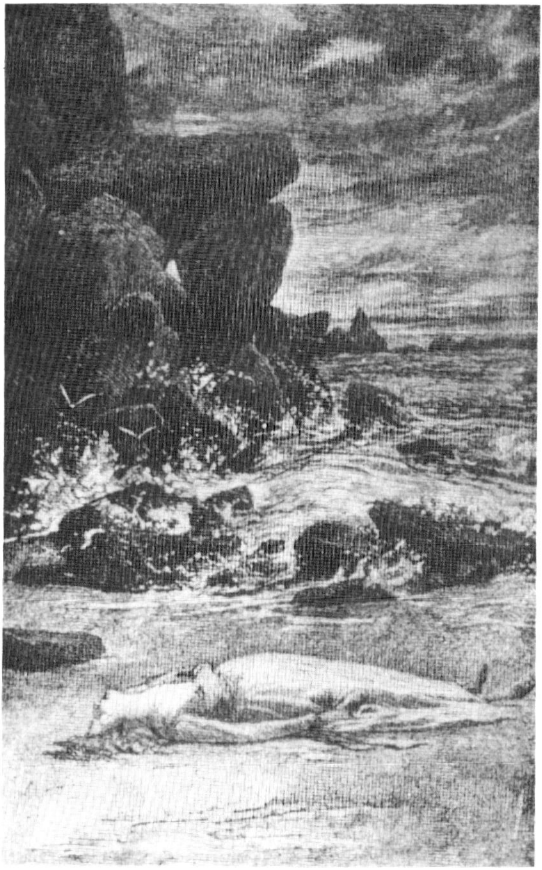

Marie who were no longer able to work, and who did not long survive their mistresses.

As for poor Fidèle, he had died of weariness about the same time as his master.

I took Madame de La Tour to my house, where she held out amid such cruel losses with incredible fortitude. She had comforted Paul and Marguerite to the last as if she had been born to relieve affliction. When she had ceased seeing them, she spoke of them to me as of dearly loved friends who lived in the neighbourhood. However, she only survived them by a month. As for her aunt, far from reproaching her for her woes, she prayed to God to pardon her and to relieve the state of mental confusion into which we heard that she had fallen immediately after sending Virginie away with such cruelty.

That heartless relative did not long endure the punishment of her callousness.

On the arrival of successive vessels, I learnt that she was disturbed by a morbid depression which made life and death equally unbearable. At times, she reproached herself for the untimely end of her charming grand niece and the death of her mother, which had ensued. At other times, she congratulated herself on having rejected far from her two miserable creatures, who, she said, had disgraced her name by the baseness of their passions. Sometimes, running into a fury at the sight of the throng of worthless creatures with whom Paris is crowded, she would exclaim : "Why not send these loafers to perish in our "colonies ?" She would add that the notions of humanity, virtue, religion, espoused by all peoples, were nothing but devices imagined to suit the schemes of their kings. Then, throwing herself headlong into the opposite extreme, she gave way to superstitious fears which filled her with deadly terrors. She would hasten to bring plentiful alms to wealthy monks who were her spiritual advisers, entreating them to pacify the Divinity by the sacrifice of her fortune : as if the riches which she had denied to the poor would be agreeable to the Father of mankind ! Her imagination often conjured up fields of fire, burning mountains, where hideous spectres roamed, calling upon her with loud screams. She would throw herself down at the feet of her advisers, and she imagined tortures and torments directed against her; for Heaven, just Heaven, inspires frightening beliefs in the minds of the cruel.

Thus, she spent several years, atheistic and superstitious in turns, holding in abhorrence death and life alike. But what brought to a conclusion such a lamentable existence was the very subject to which she had sacrified the love of nature. She was distressed at the thought that her fortune would devolve, after her death, upon relations whom she hated. She consequently sought to alienate the best part of it, but these relatives, taking advantage of the fits of depression to which she was subject, secured her admission as a mental patient to an asylum, and the appointment of a custodian for her property. So that her riches themselves consummated her ruin; and, as they had hardened the heart of the one who owned them, they perverted, likewise, the heart of those who coveted them. So she died, and, to crown her misfortune, she was sufficiently lucid to understand that she was being despoiled and despised by the very persons whose counsel had guided her during all her life.

By the side of Virginie, at the foot of the same reeds, her friend Paul was buried, and, around them, their loving mothers and their faithful servants. No marble slab was erected on their lowly mounds, and no inscription engraved to record their virtues; but their memory lives on indelible in the heart of those who benefited by their charity. Their shades have no need for the glare which they had shunned in their lifetime; but, if they still take an interest in what happens on earth, no doubt, they like to wander beneath the roofs of thatch where industrious virtue resides, to comfort poverty discontented with its fate; to nourish in the heart of young lovers a lasting flame, a taste for the blessings of nature, the love of work and the fear of riches.

Public opinion, which is silent with regard to monuments erected for the glorification of kings, has attributed to some parts of this island, names which immortalize the loss of Virginie. Near *Ile d'Ambre*, amid reefs, is a passage called *La Passe du St. Géran*, named after the vessel which foundered while bringing her back from Europe.

The tip of this long promontory that you see, three leagues away, half covered by the waves, and round which the *Saint Géran* could not sail on the eve of the hurricane, to enter the harbour, is called *Cap Malheureux;* and here in front of us, at the end of this vale, is *La Baie du Tombeau*, where Virginie was found buried in the sand, as if the sea had meant to bring her body back to her family and grant last rites to her modesty on these very shores which she had honoured by her innocence.

Young lovers, bound to each other with such deep affection ! unfortunate mothers ! dear family ! these woods which provided shade for you, these fountains which flowed for your delight, these hillocks where you used to repose, all to this day mourn your loss.

No one, after you, has dared cultivate this waste, nor restore these humble huts. Your goats have run wild, your orchards are ruined, your birds have fled, and the only audible cries are those of hawks circling above this hole of rocks.

As for me, from the time when I have ceased seeing you, I am like a friend who is left friendless, as a father who has lost his children, as a traveller who wanders about on earth, alone and forgotten.

With these words, the kind old man departed,

shedding tears, and mine had flowed more than once in the course of this melancholy tale.